Heart of the Streets

Chenae Glaze

GLAZE

Dedication

This book is dedicated to all of my angels: DeAndre "Spectacula" Adams, Jonathan "Jbrooks" Brooks, Kenny "K-Mac" McKinley, Dejanirra "D.J." Elrod and Rayon "Trill Gottem" Brown. Fly high ya'll and keep a close watch.

GLAZE

Acknowledgements

I first want to give all praise and honor to God. Thank you for seeing little ol' me! Thank you for your love, grace, forgiveness, mercy, peace, joy and of course your many blessings! I'm so grateful that you chose to save me and my heart and soul belongs to you!

To my family and friends: No matter the distance between us I want you to know I love you! And I want to encourage you to push through whatever you have to, to reach your destiny! Choose God and hold on to His unchanging hand. He will do it!

Last but not least I want to thank myself for pushing through every obstacle, fighting every ounce of procrastination, turning a deaf ear to everyone who said I couldn't, wouldn't or shouldn't and finishing what I started. I love you girl! (Hi-fives self)

GLAZE

<u>Prelude</u>

I'm dying. God please! I'm dying. This can't be how it ends. God, I haven't lived yet! I can't go like this...Please God, Please!
Corinne's bullet riddled body lay in a pool of blood and shattered glass.
Get up Corinne. Get up. You have to get up.
The chill from the tiles on the floor began to make her shiver and her breathing became shallow.
Not like this Corinne! Get yourself together. Get Up! Get Up!
She gathered enough strength to turn on her side but what she saw caused more pain than the four bullets that had ripped her flesh apart. Less than four feet from her body was his, bloody and still. All of a sudden the room became cold and hard.

"Baby! Baby! Jabari please open your eyes!" she tried to scream, "Open your eyes baby!" she pleaded tearfully.

God please don't do this. Please don't let him be dead. Please don't let me die. God please!

With the smell of gun powder burning her nose, Corinne inched her way to Jabari's motionless body with every movement causing more and more affliction. After what seemed like an eternity she was finally close enough to lay her head on his blood spattered chest.

"Jabari baby please just open your eyes! Please!" she begged.

The smell of burnt flesh clouded her nostrils, overtaking the gun powder smell of the room. Corinne could feel Jabari's warm blood ooze from his chest beneath her tear stain cheeks. She inched closer to his face to see if she could see a sign of life. Nothing.

Please God let there be a heartbeat.

Boom Boom.....Boom Boom.... It was weak but it was there. She closed her eyes.

God please!

There was a faint sound.

God please!

The sound became clearer.

"Corinne," he struggled to get out, "Corinne."

"I'm here baby! Please open your eyes. Just let me see your eyes!"

Jabari's eyes began to flutter and slowly opened. He mustered enough strength to look at his love for what felt like would be the last time.

"I'm...I'm sorry...I'm so sorry," Jabari said through clenched teeth. His pain seemed unbearable.

"Don't apologize baby please just hold on. It's me and you till the end right?"

He shook his head with an expression of agony written across his face.

"Well this ain't our end! Hold on Jabari please!" Corinne pleaded.

Corinne began to pray.

God please help us. I'm sorry God....we're sorry! Please don't let it end like this. If you spare us from this death God my life is yours! I promise God, I promise.

Corinne felt movement. Jabari's hand had found hers like many times before and they held on to each other. However, something was very different about this time; they were holding on for dear life.

Chapter 1: Corinne

The day had finally rolled around that I had been dreading and ironically everything about it was perfect. It was Friday, the skies were blue and the temperature was ideal. However, I still couldn't seem to get myself out of bed. I laid there staring out the window wishing it was over already.

Ring. Ring. Ring. The house phone lit up on the nightstand.

Who is this already? Aunt Renee.

Ring. Ring. Ring.

Nope. I won't deal with her shit today.

Ring. Ring. Ring.

Please God let her get the damn hint. I don't wanna talk!

Ring. Ring. Ring.

"Yes?!?" I answered irritated, "Yes, Aunty Renee?"

"Why you sound like that hunny? I was just checking on you," she responded not hiding that she was offended.

"Well for one it ain't even 9am and you done called 3 times in a row."

"I just wanted to make sure you were okay. You know today makes two years and..."

"How could I forget what today is Aunty Renee," I interrupted, "She was my mother!"

Click.

The tears streamed down my face as I threw myself under the covers. My mother had been dead for two years now and my aunt's call to remind me of the worst day of my entire life pissed me off.

She don't call to say how you doing? You need anything? But she calls to remind me that you're gone! AAAHHHHH! I just wish you were here! Why'd you leave me Mama? I thought to myself angrily.

My mother Maurion died August 1, 2006, after a yearlong battle with Ovarian Cancer. I was 16 and the only child and the relationship my mother and I shared was remarkable. We were best friends and each other's confidants. My father, Cory, left us when I was 6 years old. He got married, had more kids, and made Mama and I a distant memory. Mama didn't let it faze her though; she worked two jobs and still had time to make sure I didn't feel his absence. She took on the role of both parents like so many other single mothers around her had to do. I didn't want for anything, matter of fact I had more than most of my cousins and friends from the neighborhood. We spent our weekends together no matter how many hours Mama had worked that week. We enjoyed movies, shopping, picnics in the park, our Saturday morning hair appointments, and my favorite: girl's night. We would paint each other's nails, give massages, and get lost in hours of girl talk. We would talk about any and everything. I would fill her in on the happenings around school, the boy I had a crush on, or what I hoped for in college. Mama would give me her full attention and give me advice. She didn't believe in sugar coating things because she didn't want me to be surprised when it was my turn to experience life. She supported my ideas and pushed me to claim and go get the things I desired. Mama was a God fearing woman. She prayed, read her Bible daily and fasted weekly. She taught me to have a relationship with God at a young age.

She would always say, "Corinne always keep God first in everything you do baby and in every decision you make. Let Him order your steps and you will never go wrong."

I loved my Mother with ever breath in my body and life was amazing until that fateful day when a sharp pain became so much more. After her diagnosis, I took care of her just like she had done for me my whole life. I took her to every chemo sessions, clothe, fed, and bathe her. I became the caregiver to the only person that I felt cared and loved me.

On the eve before my mother died, she instructed me to remove an envelope from her nightstand. The envelope simply read:

For you when I'm gone.

I'm too young God. Please don't take my mama!
My knees became weak. *When I'm gone.* I had
never pictured life without Mama and the
thought crippled me with pain. I grabbed my
mother and held her like she use to do me when
I was a small child. I cried. She smiled. And we
fell asleep. The next morning I found out the
true meaning of alone. She had gone to be with
her Lord.

The week after my mother died is still a blur.
There were many sad faces, hugs, and definitely
empty promises. I stayed to myself and held on
tightly to the last piece of my mother that I had.
I tried to bring myself to read it every day but
each time I failed. It wasn't until the evening
after my Mother's funeral that I found the
courage to open the envelope. As I lay on
Mama's bed, I traced the beautiful penmanship
with my fingertips. I smelled the paper trying to
pick up the sweet vanilla scent that she loved to
wear. There was a faint hint. I hugged the
papers for what seemed like forever just wishing
I could hug her one more time. After about an
hour I was finally ready to read Mama's last
words....

Dear My Sweet Corinne,

The words on the paper brought so much pain
and joy at the same time. I could feel her
presence all around me and hear her voice as I
read the page; the tears fell uncontrollably.

I love you so much baby and I'm so sorry I had
to leave you so soon. I was tired but now I'm
resting and you no longer have to worry about
me Corinne. This time apart is only for a little

while and as long as you keep your eyes on God Corinne we'll be together again. I am so proud of the young woman you have blossomed into before my eyes. As you come fully into womanhood remember all the things I taught you. Remember all the lessons and all of the conversations. Let them guide you along the way. Keep God first in every decision you make Corinne and your journey will be easier. Stay true to yourself and to those you come to love. When you have children of your own love them as the gifts from God they are and be the example you want them to follow. I am sorry I won't be there to coach you through these things but I'll be there in spirit. I live in your heart Corinne; I am apart of you baby. I know these days will be tough but hold your head high. Smile when you can. Don't let your grief control you Corinne because it can ruin lives. I love you more than these words could ever explain.

As I neared the end of the letter I saw something that made my blood boil with anger. The conclusion was signed:

I'll always be with you!
Your Loving Mother,
Maurion Jackson
P.S. Don't let go of God's unchanging hand.

Let Go of His hand? Naw He let go of mine when He took you from me.......

I shook myself from the painful walk down memory lane only to find myself still lying in bed. I could hear the lyrics from Usher's Moving Mountains coming from under the covers followed by a brief vibration. I pulled the covers back and grabbed my cell phone.

"Hello!?!" I answered annoyed.

"Damn Cee it's like that? Mama must've been calling all morning?" He chuckled.

It was my cousin Bubba; my Aunt Renee's son. He was the only family member I had that kept his promise to be there after Mama's funeral.

"Oh my bad boy...yeah she done called a couple of times this morning. She call herself reminding me of what today is. I know what today is and when everybody else forgets I'll be the one who can never forget!" I said angrily into the phone.

There was a silence and I knew Bubba was looking for the right words.

"My bad...I don't know why Mama do that. You okay though?"

"Yeah I'm good Bubba." I lied.

"Corinne...You know I know you."

"I'm good Bubba," I stressed, "I mean I'll get through it."

"I know cuz...I just hate seeing you down but you say you good then you good. Look though, I'm having a dice party at the crib tonight. Everybody comin' through so you might as well get out that house and come kick it with ya cuz. And Cee don't try to play me 'cause you know I pull up on you," Bubba said jokingly.

I laughed for the first time that day.

"I know your crazy ass will. I have to be at work at 2 o'clock though and I don't get off till 9:00. You picking me up or I gotta catch the bus?" I said sarcastically knowing he wasn't going for that.

Bubba hated when I rode the bus. He always offered to buy me a car or fussed about me working enough to be able to get my own. To me it was about more than a car though. Mama and I were supposed to pick out my first car together. Every time I decided to go to a car lot the pain of doing something without her broke me down. It was just easier to catch the bus and avoid the grief.

"You really gone try me like that? I know today be havin' you throwed off and shit but if you try me like that again it's gone be me and you."

"Whateva Bubba get off my line!" I said laughing "I'll be there at 9pm on the dot. Bring enough clothes for the whole weekend 'cause I ain't bringin' you back till Sunday." He instructed. Click.

I looked at the phone and smiled.

This nigga just hung up on me and he don't even know if I gotta work this weekend or not to be tellin' me to pack a damn bag.

I loved my cousin Bubba; he was like the brother I never had. He was only a year older than me and I looked up to him. Bubba was the oldest of my Aunt Renee's 7 sons and even though he was surrounded by siblings he knew what it felt like to be alone. The man he had always known as his father left when Bubba was 7, ironically around the same time my dad did. Turns out Aunty Renee was a lil loose back in her day and one way or another Uncle Charles, as I had always called him, found out Bubba wasn't his. After Unc left, Aunty Renee began to resent and blame Bubba for her foolish mistake and loneliness. Mama always said it was a shame how she treated Bubba and that one day he would be the one she needed. Mama would often come to Bubba's rescue and let him stay at our house if things blew up to bad at Auntie's house. She even offered him permanent refuge but he refused. He wouldn't leave his brothers there to fend for themselves. Heroic. Over the years Bubba learned how to deal with Aunt Renee's resentment by staying out her way. What she took out on him he took out on the streets. He turned his frustration and hurt into ambition and he flipped and jugged whatever he got his hands on. Bubba could sell you the socks off somebody else feet if he wanted to. He was a true hustla and he moved whatever "product" was selling the fastest at the time. Bubba was determined to take care of his brothers. He figured, if he took on the financial role that his brother's fathers had left void his mama would love him again. But when my mother died Aunt Renee's grief along with her resentment created an even bigger drift between them and one night everything hit the fan. I still don't know the details of the argument because Bubba never speaks about it but from that night on the streets became his home; his family.

The loneliness that Bubba and I felt drew us closer together and our bond became unbreakable. He was the only family member that checked on me daily; he was my protector. He had his issues, hell I had mine but we continued to be each other's shoulder.

Beep. Beep. Beep.

The alarm on my phone broke up my thoughts. *11:00am.* It was time for me to get out the bed and get ready for work. I had to face this God forsaken day head on.

After Mama died I was bounced around from family member to family member but it felt like stranger to stranger. No one knew how to console me so my grief became a burden and no one wanted me around for long periods of time. I found comfort and peace in schoolwork and after graduation I found the same in the workforce. My job became my therapy, a place where I could forget the pain of home wherever that was at the moment. The last couple of months it had been my cousin Kelly's house. She was a single work-a-holic that was never home and when she was, she slept.

I was an employee at Pets-R-Us, a family owned pet store. I had been there for two years, had never missed a day and almost always worked overtime. It wasn't until recently that management decided to shake things up and for the first time in two years I was given a weekend off. Of all weekends this weekend! Before Bubba called I didn't know what I was gone do with myself I just knew that I didn't want to be alone.

I snapped out of my thoughts as I felt a hint of excitement creep up. I was finally getting out the house and I smiled as I got up and looked out the window. Kelly wasn't home. I walked over to the dresser and opened the top drawer. I touched the envelope mama left and tears immediately began to form.

For you when I'm gone....

I replayed those words over and over in my head and didn't even notice the walk to the bathroom. I was stuck in a daze; stuck in the pain.

C'mon Corinne. Get it together. Don't let it take hold. You have to make it to work. Keep it together.

I looked in the mirror and the eyes of a broken soul stared back. I looked myself over. My almond brown hair came just below my shoulders and was tucked neatly behind my ears. I had always prided myself on my healthy, naturally long hair plus it complimented my caramel complexion well. I had always gotten compliments about how pretty I was too and how beautiful my smile was. Today I didn't feel it though. I tried to muster up a smile but couldn't see the beauty that everyone else saw.

Get it together Corinne.

I began to undress while staring at my 5 ft. body in the mirror. I had a cute, petite figure. No stretch marks, flat stomach, toned legs and plenty of tattoos. I had acquired a fetish for ink over the last two years. The pain took me somewhere else and I was up to fifteen. I ran my hand across the tattoo that covered my side.

"I wonder what's next and where?" I thought aloud.

My thoughts were interrupted by the second alarm on my phone.

11:30am.

The water from the shower is a tricky little something. It tends to amplify whatever emotion you are feeling at the time. If you're happy the shower water will have you singing your heart out. In my case, the water turned on the faucets I called my eyes. I was crying uncontrollably.

"Mama I need you!" I screamed, "I need you so bad!"

Get it together Corinne. Pull yourself together.

I gave myself a pep talk as I showered and dressed. If I didn't get it together now my day would be controlled by my pain. I learned that the pain never goes away, I missed my mother every day, but the key was not allowing the pain to dictate my days or I would be a basket case.

I got out the shower, dressed, and went down to the kitchen. I immediately missed the wonderful smells that use to come from Mama's kitchen. She never missed a day of cooking me breakfast and dinner no matter what was going on. She was a true superwoman and I realized too late that I had taken those things for granted.

Mama made sure I had skills in the kitchen too. She would always say, "You gotta know how to keep that man. Feed his mind, body, and soul Corinne. Don't no man want a woman that can't hold home down, you hear me?" That memory made me smile. Mama was a trip!

She would have me in the kitchen watching her every move.

"You don't need measuring cups Corinne, measure with your heart. Fix your food with love and you'll get it right every time."

I cherished those little lessons now, but because I had no one to cook for I ate out all the time. It felt like decades since I'd had a home cooked meal.

I grabbed a granola bar, my bag, the keys, and walked out the door. The bus would pull up at 12:30pm. It was 12:11.

Damn. 19 minutes. Hurry up Corinne.

It was hot outside with clear skies. I loved our Atlanta weather and so did the neighborhood kids. They were out in full effect enjoying their last weeks of summer.

"Hey Ms. Corinne! You finna go to work?" The Morris children yelled in unison. I kept them on occasion when their mama wanted a club fix.

"Yea ya'll and I'm late so I can't stand around. Get out the street and be good today."

"Yes Ma'am!"

The respect they gave me made me smile. I was only 18 but to them I was just as grown as they mama.

The walk down Flat Shoals to the bus stop on Old National took me 15 minutes.

12:14pm.

Please God don't let me miss this bus.

I couldn't miss the 12:30 bus and still make it to work by 2pm. I had to catch a Marta bus, the train, and then transfer to CCT just to get to work. I made my way down Flat Shoals with an extra pep in my step.

12:26pm.

4 minutes. Almost there.

I could see the 89 coming over the hill across Old National; it stopped at the IHOP. The light was red so I had time to cut through Advance Auto Part's parking lot.

I made it. Thank you God.

GLAZE

As I stood in line waiting to board the bus, I got my fare ready and put my headphones in. I was going to need all the help I could get to keep a smile on my face for the rest of this day. I knew my music would be a great way to start because it always changed my mood no matter the occasion. With my Nano playing, I sat in a window seat and gazed out. The sound of T.I's *Whatever You Like* took my thoughts to other places and I began to wonder what this weekend had in store for me.

Chapter 2: Corinne

Bzzzzz. Bzzzzz. Bzzzzz. My phone went off. It was a text from Bubba:

Im outside.

Bubba wasn't playing; it was 9pm on the dot. My life had revolved around work for the last two years and now I was finally breaking the cycle with one of Bubba's parties. I finished counting my drawer and clocked out. A smile spread across my face as I reminisced about the days before everything came crashing down. I could feel the excitement burning in the pit of my stomach and I could no longer hide it as I walked to the car. We were back at it.
"What the hell you smiling like that for?" Bubba asked as I closed the car door.

I leaned over and hugged him tight then kissed his cheek.

"Man I missed you," I said fighting the tears, "I miss the old days, I miss kickin'
shit witcha everyday. I'm sorry I pushed everybody away—"

Bubba stopped me before I could even finish.

"Come on now wit the emotional shit.
You ain't gotta apologize to me. We good. I know this shit ain't been easy for you and I know you needed ya space. I also knew you would come around in your own time. You more than
my lil cuz; you my lil suh and I'ma be here long as the good Lord allow me to be. Now
wipe ya face ol' snot nose ass lil girl." Bubba said jokingly.

He had always been the jokester of the family.

"Put ya seatbelt on so we can ride."

"For you to be so G them folks show do got you shook!" I was laughing.

"Naw aint nobody got me shook but
I aint finna give em a reason to fuck wit me either. We in Cobb girl."

We finally pulled out the parking lot and on to Cobb Parkway in traffic. I hated traffic and Bubba knew this so before I could get a complaint out he turned up the music.

"Aye you heard that new Gucci? Chicken Talk pt.2?" he asked.

"Naw I aint heard it. You got it? And how the hell is it so much traffic at this time of night!?!" I said getting irritated.

"What?!? Damn I gotta start getting yo ass out the house! This shit ridin'! Listen to this cuz!," he screamed over the bass in his '89 Caprice Classic completely ignoring my comment about the traffic. He turned off Young Jeezy's My

President is Black, a tribute to our first black president Barack Obama, and put on Gucci's song.

♪♫ *I'ma gold mouf dog definition of the South. Aint no quarters or no halves just some wholes in this house* ♪♫

The lyrics to Gucci Mane's *Swing My Door* boomed from Bubbas two 12's as we made our way to Bubba's house.

Bubba had a couple of spots of his own, two on the Southside and one in Cobb. He believed in changing it up, he wasn't gone let a nigga catch him slippin.

"Oooohhh Cee you heard what he said? *It's a lot of crack smokers in the apartments where I stay and I know they name and face cause I serve 'em everyday...*" He rapped along with Gucci Mane.

"I gotta brang that back cuz!" And he played it all the way to our destination. When we were near Bubba's house we pulled into the gas station on the corner.

"I'm finna grab some rellos cuz you want something?

"Naw I'm good." I said as I rubbed my ears; they were ringing from the bass.

Bubba laughed, "Im beatin down the block ain't I?

"Yea you doin ya thang," I reassured him.

Bubba turned on Allgood Road and pulled into his apartments with his music blasted. Summer nights brought everybody out and the apartments was live. Everybody Bubba passed threw up deuces or shouted out what up. I loved it; there ain't nothing like hood love. He took the long way driving to his apartment giving me a sort of tour.

"The street we came in on we call that Front Street and the street we on is Side Street. The three other streets that run parallel to it are Second Street, Third Street and Back Street."

I soaked it all in. Since I didn't do nothing but work and sleep, the sight of everybody outside gave me a sort of high. I was looking out the window at a dice game that was going on in between two buildings when Bubba pulled up to a group of guys on what he called Second Street. They all turned around and a familiar face walked over to the car.

"What up bruh?" the guy said leaning down to look in the car. I could feel him looking at me so I looked out the window in the opposite direction.

"What up," They dapped each other up, "You coming through tonight? I'ma throw a lil dice party. I got the alcohol and the trees. It's some money coming through to get on them dice too."

"Oh yeah?" dude said looking at the screen of his phone with *Swing My Door* coming from the phone speakers.

"You got it as a ringtone?!? Damn bruh you beat me to it. I just put my lil cuz on it...oh matter fact, you remember my lil cuz Corinne? Corinne this Jabari." Bubba re-introduced. I remembered seeing him with Bubba at Aunt Renee's house a couple of times. I turned around enough to glimpse his moonlit silhouette.

"Hey." I said.

"What up?"

"Alright bruh let me get to the house and set up
'fore these folks start pullin' up. Ya'll boys come
through" They dapped up again.
Bubba parked the car around the corner and
we got out.
"What up Bubba?" one of his neighbors yelled.
"What up!"
"You the man round here ain't cha?" I asked
with a smirk on my face.
"Naw cuz I aint the man, I'm just me. You know
the hood love me." He said while grabbing my
bags out my hand. He stopped and stared at me
for a second.
"Nigga what you staring for?" I asked feeling
awkward.
"Cause these niggas finna be choosin'. You a
new face and you pretty, that no make-up kind
of pretty. Cee don't make me have to buss one
of these niggas bout you. Hold ya tongue." He
said in a serious tone referring to my slick
mouth.
"Bubba I'm chill. Let's go in the house." I said
giving him the same tone.
He turned and started walking around the
building we were parked at.
I should have known Bubba didn't live
anywhere near where he parked.
After passing two buildings we were finally at
his house. The smell of weed and cigarettes hit
me before I even crossed the threshold of the
front door. Once inside I looked around. His
house was a typical bachelor pad: Two couches,
Flat screens in every room, and an empty dining
room.
"Why don't you have a dining room table
Bubba?"

"Cause that's the dice room cuz. The house in Shady Park got all that stuff in it....this just my spot to crash when I'm in Cobb."

"Well where I'm sleeping?"

"I got two bedrooms, come put ya stuff in here." I followed as he led the way. A bed and a flat screen was all that awaited me.

"See a nigga got home trainin'. I changed the sheets and stuff for you...Aunty Maurion taught me that."

The words stung. There was a silence as thoughts of Mama flooded our memories. We were both lost in our thoughts when Bubba's cell rung.

"What up? Yea it's still on. Y'all can come on through. Bet."

As he hung up the phone I could feel him watching me. I know he couldn't hug me in order to keep his emotions in check but he came and stood next to me.

"I'm sorry Cee. I know you miss her. I miss her too. We got each other though.

Hold ya head lil cuz and try to have a good time tonight. Figure out what you wanna do tomorrow and we'll do it, okay?"

"Alright." I struggled to get out as the tears fell.

"Im'a go in here and get stuff together, you handle ya biz and come out when you ready." I nodded. Bubba left and closed the door behind him leaving me to my tears. He had his own way of grieving, hustling, and I knew he was hurting almost as bad as I was. Mama was like his mother too.

I sat on the bed and held on to the edge. My heart was beating so fast and hard.

Mama....I need you. I miss you so much!

The tears that I held in the whole day flowed now so heavily. Bubba came in silently and brought me a bottled water. He grabbed my shoulder then left. I laid on the bed, buried my head into the pillow and cried.

I had fallen asleep and when I woke up the light was off and music was playing loudly throughout the house. Once I realized where I was I cracked the door and looked out. I could see people walking in the living room and hear what sounded like arguing coming from the dining room.

The dice game Corinne.

I closed the door and cut the light on. I looked at my phone and checked the time. 11:40pm. I had been sleep for an hour and a half. I text Bubba:

Come here please.

He came in like he was ready for war.

"What's wrong Corinne?!?"

"Nothing Bubba calm down. Why you so hype?" I said puzzled.

"Oh ok. I thought one of them niggas might of came back here. I told everybody to stay outta here. What up?" he said closing the door behind him.

"Nothing I just wanted to take a shower and change clothes before I went out there. I meant to earlier...matter fact why you let me fall asleep?"

"Man you was crying for a minute I knew you had to sleep that shit off so I left you alone. You ain't gotta ask me to take a shower though cuz."

"Nigga I know I'm just telling you 'cause I know you got people out there and just in case somebody had to use the bathroom I'm letting you know I'ma be in the shower."

"Oh damn you need a towel and a rag? I'ma have to go get you one real quick."

"Naw I brought my own...I know you a bachelor." I said with a smile.

"Alright hurry up and come kick it....The party really just startin you know niggas ain't neva on time." Bubba said as he walked out. I could see people from the living room tryna get a glimpse of who was in the room.

"Damn Niggas!" I heard Bubba say from the other side of the door. I laughed at my cousin he was crazy.

I showered and dressed, putting on a white fitted Polo shirt, some navy blue Polo shorts, then I slid my feet in a brand new pair white Polo shoes. I bought new clothes for this weekend; you never knew where you would end up with Bubba. I had this thing for lotions and smell goods too and made sure to put on my new Malibu scent from Bath and Body Works. I brushed my teeth, did a quick eyebrow arch and put on my hoops. Since I had a nice grade of hair I just used water and put my hair in a high ponytail. I laughed at myself.

Corinne who you doing all this for? I'm doin' it for you girl of course. I pointed to my reflection in the mirror.

Mama taught me about hygiene as a young girl. She would say "Corinne don't no man want no stankin' woman. Hygiene is your number one priority under God. Cleanliness is next to Godliness baby. Take care of your kit kat, as she called it, and your skin baby. Put your smell goods on if you going somewhere and put them on if you just lounging around the house.

Keep on clean panties at all times, you never know where you might end up. You don't want no doctor catching you slipping" Her ways of explaining these things always made me laugh but they've stuck with me. I smiled at those memories. I felt a lot better since I cried earlier and I was glad I was here with Bubba.
Knock. Knock. Knock.
The locked door knob rattled. I grabbed my stuff and opened the door almost bumping into Jabari.
"My bad" I said and went around him.
Something made me look back before I went in the room, the same thing must've happened to him because he was looking back too. Our eyes met and we were stuck in a brief trance for a couple of seconds. He was a very handsome man. The first thing I noticed was his razor line up and how his side burns connected to his goatee. He had a head full of waves and his jet black hair complimented his almond skin.
His Lacoste shirt fit his 5'10" frame just right making him look solid and of course I had to make sure his shoe game was up to par noticing his brand new pair of Jordan's. I broke our gaze and went in the room leaning back on the door as I closed it.
"OMG! Mama he gave me butterflies" I whispered before I could catch myself. I was actually talking to Mama out loud and it felt great for a change. I knew she couldn't talk back but that didn't mean I couldn't talk to her. I smiled, put my things in my bag and thought about that moment in the hallway with Jabari. I shook it from my head.
You're reading into nothing Corinne. I chuckled to myself.

T.I's *No Matter What* was playing when I walked
out of the room. I did a quick survey of my
surroundings. It was about 20 people in the
living room, 10 more in the breeze way, and
about 10 in the dining room and kitchen area. I
recognized a couple of faces from the South
Side. I headed to sit down and I could feel the
eyes of the girls on one of the couches watching
me. I looked at them and all but one looked
away. She had a blonde quick weave and a lip
piercing.
"What Up? I said with my eyebrow raised.
She smirked.
Let it go Corinne. She a silly hoe and
she ain't worth it.
I had a quick temper and a low tolerance for
bullshit. I gave her a look to let her know I
wasn't the one to play with then went to find
Bubba. I didn't see him in the house so I walked
out the wide open front door to see if I could see
him. He was standing out in front of his
building in the middle of a circle rapping. I
laughed. He always did think he was a rapper. I
walked up just as he was finishing his 8 bars.
"What up cuz you good?" He said walking
towards me.
I could hear whispers inquiring about me as we
walked back to the house.
"Aye cuz the drank in the kitchen and here go
you some trees to roll up. Be careful with that
though that's that thang." He said talking about
the green.
"You might can drink me under the table but I
can out smoke you any day Bubba" I said.
As we walked pass the living room the blonde
head girl watched us intensely. She was

starting to get on my nerves but I promised
Bubba I would stay cool, so I laughed at her,
took the seven ounces and a box of rellos from
him and walked to the kitchen.
*Let me get this green in my system 'fore me
and shawty have a problem.*
My tolerance for alcohol had always been low so
I didn't like to drink but the weed didn't bother
me. I started smoking heavy right after Mama
died and never had to pay for it 'cause Bubba
always had it.
I walked past the dice game and stopped to
watch. Dice had always interested me ever since
I was a little girl.
"Give me them! Them too!"
"Let me see Kobe number! Ya'll know what Kobe
number is don't y'all?"
Dice lingo was funny to me and I burst out
laughing as I went into the kitchen. There were
bottles everywhere.
What the hell, I might as well grab a drank.
I grabbed one of the red plastic cups and
poured me some vodka, cranberry, and orange
juice. On my way back to the living room the
one holding the dice turned and said,
"Damn shawty you smell good as hell."
When I turned around to respond all eyes were
on me including Jabari's.
"Thank you."
I made my way to the living room and one of the
guys sitting down scooted over to make room.
"Here you go ma."
"Thank you, you smoke?" I held up the seven
for him to see.
"Yea you finna roll up?" he asked offering me
a rello but I showed him mine.
"Yea."

I sat down and started breaking down the weed. The blonde head girl and her lil crew were looking like they wanted in on the rotation. *This broad can't possibly think she finna smoke this blunt with me.* My thoughts were quickly broken up.

"What's ya name shawty?" The one who offered the seat asked.

"Corinne."

" Kevin," he said while reaching for my hand to shake.

I shook his hand and continued what I was doing. Kevin was making small talk so I made sure to throw in a couple of for real's and uh huh's but my attention was on the dice game. I had a clear view from the couch I was on and a clear view of Jabari. It was something in his eyes that drew me to him other than his good looks. Our eyes met a couple of more times and that same feeling I had in the hallway crept in every time.

"Damn shawty you rolled the hell out that blunt." I heard Kevin say as I fired it up.

I winked at him and pulled the blunt. My rolling skills had always been a sort of hypnotizing, turn on to the street niggas I knew and Kevin wasn't exempt from the spell. We smoked and laughed together for the next couple of hours ignoring the thirsty looks from the broads on the couch next to us.

We were on blunt number four when Swing My Door came up next in the rotation and Bubba walked in the door at the same time rapping the lyrics.

"Aye that's my shit turn it up!" Bubba screamed.

He was tipsy now and ready to turn up.

♫♪ *Swing my door, swing my door, every time they swing my door, I count 18 5 every time they swing my door*♫♪

The entire house erupted in song everybody singing the lyrics. I even chimed in between puffs.

"Aye cuz I see you!" Bubba yelled, "Yea I turned you on to this shit it's ridin' ain't it?" He was dancing around the living room with his cup in hand.

"Yea cuz you did that." I responded. The weed was taking effect. I was relaxed.

"AAHHHHH! I told yo ass that was that thrax! You over there high as hell let me hit that shit Kevin," he said grabbing the blunt and he continued dancing around the living room.

Bubba was telling the truth about the green. I was stuck, tuning everything around me out, everything except the dice game and Jabari was on the dice. He had his money in one hand and dice in the other. Everything about how he rolled had my attention. He was striking and his opponent was pissed. He caught me watching, smiled and winked. The butterflies fluttered all over my body. I felt somebody sit by me and the movement took me out of my trance.

"Cuz I'm bout drunk as hell but I see you watching the dice game. Now, are you watching the game or you watching one of them niggas?" Bubba asked.

I looked around to see who heard him but everybody was either drunk or high and in their own world.

"Ain't nobody paying me no attention while you looking around. Who you watching?"

"Nigga I ain't watchin nobody...... you know I love a dice game." I tried my best to sound convincing.

"Yea my nigga over there striking them niggas. He a real nigga cuz. He had my back on some shit a while back and been one hunned since I met him."

"Who you talking bout Bubba?" I played dumb.

"You know exactly who I'm talking bout...the one you watchin." He said then got up and walked off.

This nigga know me too damn well! Thank you mama for leaving me here with somebody I know really got my back.

My eyes filled with tears.

Ok Corinne shake it off don't go there.

I had to shake those thoughts especially while I was intoxicated so I got up and walked in the kitchen. Bubba always kept snacks because he always kept the munchies. I grabbed a small bag of Cheetos, a Nutty Bar, and a Sprite. As I was walking out the kitchen Jabari was standing in the doorway with his back to me. I stood there for a second trying to figure out if I should say something or just walk by. I started moving but before I could say something he spoke.

"You got the munchies don't cha Miss Lady?"

Miss Lady. Miss Lady.mmm Miss Lady.

Something about the way he said it melted my heart like butter.

"Something like that." I said with a smile.

It must've been a huge smile because he said, "You got a big, pretty smile too."

If I was white my cheeks would've been fire engine red. I thanked him and walked as casually as I could to the bathroom. I looked in the mirror and made sure I didn't have any food in my teeth. Coast clear. I splashed my face with water and put Visine in my eyes. I hated that "high" look. When I came back into the living room I realized the crowd had dwindled down. There were only a few people hanging around and a few on the dice. I checked my phone. 4:23 am. I walked towards the couches and saw that the crew of girls had left and Kevin was sitting there alone. Kicking off my shoes I sat on the opposite couch with my feet up under me eating my Cheetos. Kevin threw me a couple of awkward glances but when he finally got up the nerve to sit by me he was met by Jabari. My heart jumped. They looked at each other, glanced at me then looked at each other again. Jabari's aura was commanding.

"It was nice meeting you Corinne," Kevin said shaking my hand. He gave a sheepish nod towards Jabari as he turned and walked out the door. As Jabari sat down next to me I stared in disbelief.

Did he just chump this nigga off with a look?!?
Mama these butterflies!

The fearless display of power turned me on in every way possible. I picked up the remote and turned the TV to the music video channel trying not to let on that I was impressed.

"You can't hear it Miss Lady with the music on."

"I know. I just wanted to look at something."

I turned and looked him in the eyes and a smile spread across his face.

Mama his lips....they're so juicy.

"You enjoyed yourself?" He asked.

"I ain't do nothing but smoke but I'm glad I came...so yeah I guess I did."

I heard people dapping up. I looked around and
the crowd had dwindled down even further.
"Alright ya'll..... I 'preciate ya'll for comin
through. Holla at me tomorrow." Bubba said.
A chubby, dark skinned man known as Fat Boy
turned around before he walked out the door,
"Aye boy what you gone do?" he was talking to
Jabari.
"Shit I'm chillin."
"Aight" He dapped Jabari up with a smile
glancing at me, "I'ma holla at cha in the
morning." He pointed to me and said "Alright
shawty," then he walked out the door.
Bubba locked the door and sat on the opposite
couch from me and Jabari.
"Cuz let me see that remote."
I threw it to him; he turned off the radio and
turned the TV up.
"Man I'm bout drunk as a fool." Bubba said
slurred.
Jabari and I both laughed but were interrupted
by a soft knock at the door.
"Well ya'll me and my lady friend bout to handle
some business and then I'm crashin'. Ya'll hold
it down."
He opened the door and there stood the broad
from earlier with the blonde quick weave.
*Oh that's why the broad was staring. She
was tryna check the scene. Silly ass girl.*
As they walked to his room she had an extra
pep in her step. Jabari looked at me and we
laughed again.
"You got something you wanna watch?" I asked
him.
"You good Miss Lady. Watch what
you wanna watch."
"Well I'ma put on one of these movies."

I walked over to Bubba's DVD collection. He
had every black movie ever made. I picked up
Vampire in Brooklyn and held it up for him to
see. Jabari nodded in approval. I put it on, sat
back on the couch and turned off the lamp next
to me.

"Aye you wanna stretch out?"

I hesitated, "Yea."

Jabari scooted down and let me stretch out on
the couch placing my feet under his thigh. After
a while I felt him get up and when he came
back he had the cover off the guest bed. He
spread it over me then sat back on his end of
the couch.

Mama he's sweet.

"Thank you."

"You good." He said with a smile.

I was high and relaxed and before long the
movie was watching me. A couple of hours after
I fell asleep Jabari came and laid behind me
putting my legs between his. He put his nose
right in the nape of my neck and wrapped his
arms around me. We slept peacefully like we
had known each other our whole lives and I felt
safe in his arms; no worries at all.

Chapter 3: Jabari

Bzzzzz. Bzzzzz. Bzzzzz.

My phone went off in my pocket. I grabbed for it as slowly as I could trying not to wake her up. I looked at the screen; it was my patna Memphis.

"What up bruh?" I said in a hushed tone.

"Wake ya ugly ass up nigga!" Memphis said.

"I'm finna get up nigga."

"Just callin' to make sure we still doin that today and what time cause I heard you was caked up and shit."

"I told bruh round two...what time is it?" I asked ignoring the comment.

"Eleven"

"Alright come round Bubba's we'll leave from here round 1:15."

"Yea."

Click.

Memphis was my right hand man. He was the first nigga I met when I came to Atlanta and his loyalty ran deep. We kept our circle small. It only included Me, Memphis, Fat Boy, Slim, Bubba and my South Side patnas Yoshi and Dough. We had our outside associates and the niggas that tried to kick it with us to make a name for themselves but them six was my main niggas...the ones that trusted me with their lives.

I put my phone back in my pocket then looked at Corinne. She was naturally beautiful with flawless soft skin. I laid back down behind her pulling her closer to me.

Damn she smells so good.

"You smell real good Miss Lady", I whispered.

"How you know I wasn't sleep? Corinne asked surprised.

"Cause you got this lil snore when you sleep."

"My bad," She said I could tell she was embarrassed, "Did it bother you?"

"Naw you good...It wasn't no loud manly snore" I said laughing.

She sat up and gave me a smile then headed to the back towards the bathroom.

She got a pretty ass smile too....

damn shawty fuckin' my head up.

It was something about Corinne's eyes and smile that drew me in. I would get lost in her gaze because it told a familiar story of pain and strength but then she would smile and the world would disappear. The stress from the streets didn't exist while I was around her; she's what I need to keep me sane. I didn't know a lot about her but I did know I wanted her...I needed her.

Chapter 4: Corinne

Jabari and I were like magnets. It had been five months since the party at Bubba's and we were inseparable. And even though we hadn't made our relationship official I had still devoted my loyalty to him. A couple of niggas that knew him had tried to holla at me but I turned them down and made sure he knew about it. I didn't want any secrets between us so I made sure I was honest and up front with him at all times. Jabari in return was there for me anytime I needed him to be. He would drive to the South Side to take me to work, pick me up and drop me back off. I cooked him diner on the nights we didn't go out to eat and he would bring me lunch to work accompanied by flowers every day. We had date night once a week, anything I wanted to do from the movies, Atlantic Station, candle lit diners, to overnight trips to the beach. What I respected the most about Jabari though was the fact that he never pressured me about

sex. I was a virgin and I wasn't ready and he respected that. I never asked him any questions about where he was getting it from either; we weren't a couple. I just simply asked that when we were together it was my time and my time only. I could talk to him about anything and we definitely talked about everything under the sun: His past, my past and where we wanted to be in the future. I opened up to him about my mama and her death and when I wasn't strong enough to talk about it he didn't force me to. He would always say, "It's ok Miss Lady you can tell me about it another time." He also opened up to me about his past and things he had never told anyone too. We were alike in many ways. All Jabari knew was the streets; they raised him. His mother died right after his delivery and he was left with his father and paternal Grandmother in South Ga. where he was born. His father was a well known drug dealer in their town 2 hours South of Macon and he taught his only son the ropes as soon as he could understand. But on Jabari's 15th birthday his father was gunned down in a hit for hire at the age of 35. It was a devastating lost for Jabari and it made him bitter inside. After his father's funeral, Jabari's grandmother shipped him to live with his aunt in Marietta, GA. for fear of Jabari following in his father's footsteps. Some things are just inevitable though. And at 15 Jabari went full force in the streets of his new town flipping whatever dope he could get his hands on and running over whoever got in his way. He had no sympathy on the streets that took the life of his father.
I didn't want to know how far he was in the dope game so I didn't ask and I think the fact

that I didn't press him about it drew him closer to me. I worked and had my own money so I didn't feel the need to ask him for his. That turned him on too and made him want to shower me in it. He knew I wouldn't ask for anything so he would put money in my drawer for me to find and I would take it and put it in a savings account. I never knew when I might need it.

After Bubba's party I put in a request to have weekends off at work. They were more than happy to oblige because I had worked 7 days a week for two years straight. I enjoyed the weekends off because it gave me time to spend with Bubba and Jabari.

It was the morning of New Year's Eve and I was cleaning up the house and listening to music when my phone rang.

"Hello?"

"What you doin' Miss Lady?"

I smiled, "Nothing, cleaning up. What you doin'?"

"On the way to get you. Get dressed we celebrating today." I could hear the excitement in his voice.

"What for New Year's?"

"For that too but I 'ma tell you when I see you. I'll be there in about 20 minutes." Jabari didn't like to talk over the phone much; he was always worried about the phone being tapped.

"Okay. The garage door gone be unlocked for you cause I gotta get in the shower."

"Yea. We gone talk about that too."

"Talk about what?"

"Nothing Corinne I'll see you in a lil bit."

"Ok. Bye"

"Yea"

Click.

I went to the garage and unlocked the garage door. They weren't automatic and we often used them to enter the house. I checked the time on my phone. 11:45. I ran upstairs and got in the shower; Jabari's 20 minutes usually meant 10, and I wasn't even lathered up good before I heard a soft knock at the door.

"Come in. I thought you said 20 minutes" I said sarcastically peeking from behind the curtain. Jabari's Sean John cologne made the hair on the back of my neck stand up. I loved the way it smelled on him. He had on a brand new pair of black and white Concords, Black True Religion jeans and a royal blue long sleeved True Religion shirt. His fresh line up was turning me on so I popped my head back in the shower and closed the curtain all the way.

"I got something for you and make sure you pack a bag cause we in the city for the weekend." He said and walked out as quickly as he came in.

I don't know how much longer I can resist him Mama. I love him.

The thought shocked me. I love him? The more I thought about it the faster my heart beat. I don't know when I fell for him but I was certain that I had.

I got out the shower and went to my room to dress. On my bed were a brand new pair of grey True Religion jeans, a black True Religion long sleeved shirt, and a brand new pair of Cool Greys. Beside the outfit were a new grey Michael Kors purse and a Helzberg Diamond box. My heart skipped a beat. I picked up the box and opened it not knowing what to expect.

Inside was a beautiful 2 carat diamond necklace that was shaped like an angel. Tears filled my eyes as Jabari walked up behind me and I tightened the grip I had on my towel. He reached around me and grabbed the box from my hands then took the necklace out. He placed the necklace around my neck and fastened it, kissing the back of my neck when he finished. Butterflies flew throughout my body as he hugged me from behind and whispered in my ear.

"You my angel Miss Lady."

I turned to face him and the tears fell on my cheeks. He kissed both eyes and wiped them away. This was the first time I felt whole since my Mother left and I couldn't contain my emotions.

"Thank you so much. Words can't explain how I'm feeling." I whispered and kissed him. He kissed me with a passion I had never felt before and before long I had to stop him.

"I'm not ready." I said looking at the floor. He lifted my chin and said,

"It ain't about that to me, *that* move is yours. Get dressed, I'll wait downstairs."

He walked out of my room closing the door behind him.

<u>Chapter 5: Jabari</u>

Today was a day for celebration. I was finally seeing the money that I had put in the work for these last 4 years and my whole team was eating. At 16 I flipped my first brick and made my first hundred thousand, I pulled in numbers that most of the niggas my age dreamed of. And now at 19 I had made my first Mil ticket. It took my old man till he was 35 to become a millionaire and then the streets took his life. The streets don't wanna see a nigga getting' money but at the rate I was going I would be a multi-millionaire before I was 21.

One thing I knew about money was it came and went and if it didn't change you, it changed the niggas around you. I loved my niggas but when it came to money I trusted nobody. Trust is what got my old man killed and something I learned to live without when I was comin' up.

GLAZE

My team knew I was getting money, I put them on, but they didn't know how much I had run my check up. I didn't want to bring confusion or jealousy in, so our checks were something we didn't discuss. If one of us needed something we were there no questions asked and every week all 7 of us put money in a safe that Bubba kept. The money was for lawyers or bail money if one of us needed it. The old man taught me proper preparation prevents poor performance so the team stayed prepared.

Today I wanted to celebrate and the first person that came to mind was Corinne; she was just so different. I was so tired of the sack chasers that always had their hand out or just wanted to be seen with me. They didn't know what loyalty was and they ran they mouth about everything. They didn't care about me, just my check and what I could do for them. They threw the ass at me without hesitation looking for me to wife 'em up. Corinne was a different breed though. I knew it from the first time I laid eyes on her in Bubba hallway. She didn't throw herself at me and she didn't ask me for nothing. On top of that when niggas tried to get at her she remained loyal to me and we weren't even exclusive. The part that got me though was when she told me she was a virgin. I didn't believe her at first because I didn't know any 18 year old virgins. I just thought she had a nigga she was hiding and didn't want to give his goods away. I found out she had promised her Mama if she couldn't wait until marriage she wouldn't have sex until she knew it was true love and shawty kept her promise. The fact that she kept her goods from me made me want her even more but I didn't press her about it. She was beautiful inside and out and I was going to make sure I would be the first and only man to feel her insides.

The more time I spent with Corinne the more I realized she stayed true to her word and that her loyalty ran just as deep as mine. I had asked around town about her and sent a couple of niggas to try her but she turned every one of them down. I had to make sure she was what she said she was, loyal. I had already trusted her with my past but now I was ready to trust her with my heart and my money. My old man always said "The one that's loyal to you son without the relationship and the benefits is the one you wife.....and if she don't ask for nothing give her the World." I wanted to give Corinne the World.

A creak in the stairs made me snap out of my thoughts. When she came into the living room her scent filled the room; I loved the way she smelled. Her skin was always clear and smooth and I liked that she didn't wear weave. She had a body that could outshine any video vixen any day hands down. She was bad.

Corinne walked over to me and gave me a hug. "Thank you so much Jabari..... for everything." She hugged me tighter.

It felt good to be appreciated. I decided right then to make her mine.

"I was gone ask you later but I wanna know now."

"What you wanna know?" The way she said it turned me on.

"You rockin wit me right?"

"Yea you know that."

"Well I want you to rock with only me"

She looked me square in the eyes, "I been rocking with only you Jabari...you on the other hand..... Are you ready to rock with only me?"
That damn female intuition.
Corinne didn't question me about where I laid my head or about other women and I see now it wasn't because she didn't suspect it.
"Loyalty mean just as much to me as it does to you Jabari. You make me happy and I love..... being around you but my heart isn't to be played with. If you can promise to give me the same loyalty that I'm giving you I promise to rock with you through whatever."
I couldn't blame shawty for her hesitation matter of fact I appreciated her honesty. Her cousin Bubba showed her the game and he had hella hoes so I knew she figured that's how the game went. The fact that she didn't jump at the offer and stood her ground made me want her even more. I was done with the outside hoes, I wanted Corinne and her love and loyalty was worth it.
"I promise Miss Lady."
Damn I want her bad.
She must've been thinking the same thing because her next words gave my manhood strength. She leaned in and whispered in my ear, "Do you promise not to rush?" then she kissed my earlobe. I leaned back and looked at her.
She beautiful and she mine.
I thought as I ran my fingers through her hair.
"I promise to take all the time you need."
Her hands began to shake softly; she was nervous. I stood up and pulled her up to me then kissed her forehead. I wrapped my arms

around her clasping my hands in the small of her back.

"I'm ready," she whispered.

The decision I had waited so patiently to hear had finally arrived but it no longer mattered; I now had her heart and her loyalty.

Corinne told me previously how her mama told her whenever she did have sex to make sure she was in her own house. How she better not ever disrespect herself or someone else's house like that. I knew she wouldn't make a move in her cousin house and I didn't want it here either. It would be Corinne's first time and I was gone make sure it was special. Females were always sentimental about those kinda things.

"C'mon Miss Lady lets ride," I said leading her to the door.

"Wait I gotta grab my bag and my purse. I love it by the way and you ain't never tell me where we was going or what we celebratin'."

"We gone talk about it in the car." I said as she walked back up the stairs. I walked out the house and started up the car. I had copped a brand new black Mercedes C-Class the morning before and this would be her first time seeing it. She came out the house and when she saw the car a smirk formed across her mouth.

"Flexed up ain't you?" She said closing the door.

"Just a lil somethin' somethin' I picked up for us yesterday."

"For *us*?"

"Yea ....*us*. You my girl now Corinne and what's mine is yours."

"So you just knew I was gone be your girl huh?" she said laughing.

"You slick already was my girl we just ain't have a title."

She smiled and reached for the radio.

"Hold up Miss Lady. We always ride to what you wanna listen to it's my turn today."

"I guess that's fair...what you wanna listen to baby?"

Damn that shit sound so good coming from her. Shawty didn't know it but she had me gone. I was treading in unfamiliar territory with her and I wasn't resisting.

"We ridin' some Ol'School Atlanta today."

I grabbed my Outkast Atliens CD out the middle console, put it on then turned to number six and let *Elevators* flooded the speakers. It was nice as hell out for January and today we was gone put on in the city.

"You hungry?" I asked her.

"Yes. I'm kinda in the mood for some soul food. What you want?"

"It's on you."

"Okay yea that's what I want."

"Aight. I know a lil spot on Cascade."

We rode up Old National towards I-285 with Outkast's Elevators playing; Corinne knew all the lyrics.

"This ya jam ain't it?" I laughed admiring her beauty.

"Yea I love this song! You the one don't know nothing about it," She smiled and continued singing.

After the song went off Corinne reached over and turned the radio down.

"Jabari?"

"What up?"

"You said we were celebrating today...what we celebrating?"

I looked over at her not knowing how to let her in on something I had always kept to myself.

"Corinne in our relationship loyalty and trust are important. I gotta know you got my back at all times. Do you know how I get money?" She looked at me with a puzzled look.

"I know you don't punch no clock Jabari. Your phone constantly ringing but you don't stand on a corner so I figure you ain't a nickel and dimer. For the last three months you been puttin at least 9,000 dollars a week in my drawer and once a week you take a trip to South Ga. You don't talk over the phone about nothing which to me means you watching for the Feds. I don't ask what you move but I know you moving weight. I just figured when you trusted me enough you would let me in." she said casually. Shawty had me amazed. She paid attention to the details and I liked that because paying attention to the details kept you from being finessed.

"You don't think I trust you?" I asked

"I think you do to a certain extent but Jabari if you fully trusted me we wouldn't be having this conversation. I truly believe trust is earned and loyalty is shown so I guess I can show you better than I can tell you. I understand though, in your lifestyle you can't trust everybody."

"Miss Lady I trust you that's why we *are* having this conversation. Matter of fact I haven't ever trusted anyone except my grandmama the way I trust you. You my girl and I trust your loyalty and to prove it I'ma trust you with something I ain't never trusted nobody with."

I pulled around the back of The Beautiful, one of Atlanta's best soul food restaurants, and parked. I turned the car off and looked Corinne in the eyes; I needed her to understand how serious I was.

"You pay attention to details...I love that cause in this game the details matter. You right about a couple of the things you said....." I paused and looked out my window then in the rearview. I could never be too careful plus I was trying to get my thoughts together.

"I do move weight; keys and pounds to be exact." I looked at her intently to see if I could read any form of nervousness. Nothing. I continued.

"I don't have to stand on a corner 'cause I don't break nothing down. I supply my team with the product they break it down and move it around the city. We got a trap in Cobb, a trap on the South Side and I make plays in South Ga. I only deal with my team when it come to work. They get the work off and I collect what's mine at the end of the week. I don't talk on the phone about nothing...nothing Corinne. That's how I managed to stay under the radar this long."

I stopped talking to let Corinne gather her thoughts. Her face was expressionless.

"What you thinking 'bout Miss Lady?"

"I'm just letting it all soak in."

She turned her body fully facing me putting her back against the passenger door.

"So basically you the plug?" Corinne asked.

She knew more than I thought; I knew Bubba was behind that.

"Yea you can say that."

"And you only serve Bubba, Memphis, Slim and Fat Boy?"

"Yea Yoshi and Dough too...only my team."

"That's smart cause if something go wrong you know where it came from...."

I love the way she think. She got the mind of a hustla...I'ma have to thank my boy for this one.

"That's why I move like that. I treat these streets like a game of chess and my freedom and life are my King and Queen. Gotta protect them by any means necessary."

"And what about my life?" She asked looking me square in the eyes.

"I'll protect it with mine. Corinne I'll never put you in harm's way and I'll do whatever it takes to make sure you straight at all times." The thought of something happening to her because of these streets had me on edge.

"If I ask you not to make a certain move or go a certain place I need you to understand that it's for your safety. I ain't tryna be ya daddy but it's my job to make sure you straight, Aight?"

"Okay."

The car got silent. We were both lost in our own thoughts when her phone rang.

"Hello? Hey babe. Me and the boo getting something to eat. You know I am...who else I'ma be talkin bout? Yea we official now," she looked at me and smiled, "I don't know you gotta ask him. Okay love you too. Bye."

"Bubba said he bout to call you but can you answer me now that we done cleared everything else up?"

"Answer you about what Corinne?"

"What are we celebrating?"

I was more comfortable letting her in now. I leaned my head back against the headrest and it rolled right off my tongue.

"I made my first Mil."

She tilted her head and just stared at me. I couldn't read her at that moment.

"Why you lookin like that?"

"How'd you run it up like *that*?" she asked. I laughed.

"I set a goal and stayed down. I ain't run out and buy I just flipped my product and put up the profit. I ignored the safe and hustled like what was in my pockets was my last. I didn't broadcast my check and I ain't flashy. I stayed under the radar. My operation is airtight and I make sure my team eat so there ain't no greed."

"I know niggas that's been selling drugs for at least 10 plus years and they ain't seen a mil yet; it only took you 5?"

"Guarantee them niggas buy as soon as they see a profit and probably trick they money off. I told you Miss Lady these streets is like chess. Gotta make ya next move ya best move."

"And you chose to share it with me? Why?" She wasn't holding back and she didn't hesitate on asking what she wanted to know.

"Cause you don't ask for nothing and your loyalty speaks for itself. You a different breed and you deserve the world." I said.

"Well how you plan on staying in the millions? You gone take this mil and flip it in the dope game? What if you take a loss? I think you should invest some of it in something that's gone keep the money flowing in regardless. The dope game don't stay good forever."

She was a natural born hustla and a thinker. She saw beyond the million and went straight to how we can make more millions. I just looked at her and smiled; I knew I had chosen the right one.

"I like the way you think ....I already thought about everything you just said and I got that planned out but first thing first. Now that I done ran my check up where I want it....

I wanna move out the hood....and I want you to come with me."
She tensed up and looked out the windshield.
"You mean move in together?" I nodded,
"I ain't never lived with a man Jabari." She said.
"I mean I done spent the night with hoes but I ain't never lived with a woman neither other than my grandmamma." I replied.
The car got silent again. I stared at her trying to read her mind but she just stared out the window in deep thought. She was probably going over a conversation in her head she had had with her mama. She did that a lot when she had to make a decision. I never got a chance to see what having a mama was like but kickin it with my patna 'nem mamas made me wonder. I knew how much I loved my grandmamma so I figured it was something like that. I couldn't even begin to imagine life without the one person that had always been in my corner so I supported Corinne in any way she needed when it came to her Mama. Even if it meant letting decisions be made from the grave.
I came out of my thoughts and looked at Corinne. She meant to whisper to herself but I heard her say, "Mama always said a man ain't gone buy the whole cow if he can get the milk for free."
I grabbed her thigh and gave a small squeeze. "Corinne I got you. It's me and you from now on. I wanna give you the world...will you let me?"
Damn I love shawty. She ain't gone want for nothing.
She leaned over and kissed me. I slid my seat back, pulled her on to my lap, and wrapped my arms around her. At 19 I had experienced every

type of female but I had never loved any of 'em. None of them had ever made me feel like I could love them more than the streets. Then Corinne came along and stole my heart right from under me and I wasn't sharing her.

"It's me and you from here on out?" she said laying her head on my shoulder.

"Me and you."

She sat up and kissed me again.

"Okay then. I will."

I could feel her hands shaking as she climbed back in her seat. She was just as nervous as I was.

"Im in love with you Jabari" she said with her mouth and eyes and I knew she meant it, "Not because of the material things you have but because you found a way to make me feel whole again. I didn't think that was possible. When I'm with you I feel like the only girl in the world and I wanna thank you for that. And please don't say it to me because I said it to you. I'm not telling you so you can tell me....i just wanted you to know."

"You love me Miss Lady?" The thought alone gave me a rush as she shook her head yes, "I love you too Corinne."

Those words sealed the deal for me. Corinne was my Bonnie, my ride or die, and we was gone rock forever. I was gone make sure of it.

<u>Chapter 6: Corinne</u>

Mama I told him! I can't believe it...I told him.
Telling Jabari I loved him for the first time gave
me butterflies like never before. He was the only
man, that wasn't a family member; I had ever
said those words to. It felt so strange yet sweet
at the same time. I was in love and I didn't care
who knew it.

"Can we go eat now?" I said realizing we were
still sitting in the car.

Jabari unlocked the doors and came around
and opened my door. He didn't let me open
doors when we were together under any
circumstance which surprised me coming from
a nigga like him but I loved the respect.

"Why you so quiet baby?" I said as we walked
through the doors of the restaurant. He hadn't
said a word since we exchanged I love you's.

He blinked his eyes as if he was shaking his thoughts and smiled. I couldn't help but admire how handsome he was.

"Just thinking."

"About what?" I asked adding a playful smile.

"About you loving me and how I wanna be the only man you ever love." He said as he hugged me from behind while we walked to our table. I could feel myself melting in his arms.

Mama this is the best feeling.

As we ate our food and enjoyed each other's conversation I couldn't help but wonder about the million Jabari said he had. Money like that came with power but it also came with hate. People feared Jabari in the streets this I knew but if word got out about him sitting on millions how long would it be before they started plotting. I wanted to talk to him about it right then but I didn't want to spoil the moment for him so I left it alone.

Later Corinne. Tell him later.

Jabari's' phone rang interrupting our conversation.

"What up? Shit kickin it wit my girl. Yea. I told you she was gone be mine," he looked at me and winked, "We at The Beautiful right now we probably gone go shut one of these malls down in a minute. Yea. We in the Chevys tonight. Probably Echelon. Aight I'ma hit you when we leave here."

He hung up the phone and filled me in on the plans for the evening.

"We goin shoppin to pick up outfits for tonight. Guess we'll bring in the New Year at Upper Echelon."

"They gone be taxin ain't they?" Atlanta clubs raised the prices for any little thing.

"They probably will but that ain't got nothing to do with us. We don't pay to get in clubs, our face cards good."

"Nigga you think you the man don't you?" I said with my nose turned up laughing.

"Naw you think I am though."

We laughed and finished eating. As we were heading out the door a woman walked from behind the counter towards us. She looked to be in her mid 40's and had a gapped tooth smile.

"Heeeyyy baby!!!" She greeted loudly hugging Jabari.

"Hey Ms. Kay."

"I said I know he ain't gone come in here and not speak! How you been baby...who this.... ya lady friend?"

"My bad Ms. Kay you know I ain't gone forget about you. Yea this my girl Corinne. Corinne this Ms. Kay."

"Hey." I said reaching my hand out to shake hers but she pushed my hand away and hugged me.

"Ms. Kay don't shake no hands baby. Give me a hug! She show is pretty Jabari and she smell real good. What that is baby?"

I was laughing so hard inside at how animated she was.

"It's called Malibu and thank you so much."

"He treating you right cause if he ain't I'll buss him in his head." She said playfully swatting at him.

"Yes ma'am."

"Ooooh she respectful too you betta keep her!"

"Oh yea you know I got to Ms. Kay. We finna get up outta here though." He hugged her.

"Ok baby ya'll don't be no stranger and the next time I see y'all I want an invite to the wedding." I smiled and gave her a hug. "Okay see you next time."

As we walked to the car Jabari looked at me and said, "I had to cut her off.... Ms. Kay woulda had us in there all day. She'll talk you to death if you let her."

I laughed. "Who is she?"

"She use to live in the apartments. She use to cover for me back in the day when I was running around hot in the streets and keep me fed. Let me use her house to cook my work so I kept her rent paid. She use to be like a lil mama figure."

When he said that I realized he had no idea what it felt like to have a love other than street love. Everybody around him loved him for what he had or what he was doing for them in the streets. I had to show him different. I remember Mama telling me when I fell in love I would know because no circumstance or situation would change how I felt. If he never made another dime I would still love him. My love for him was unconditional. I wanted him to know but how could I show him because telling him was easy.

Jabari's phone conversation pulled me out of my thoughts.

"What up boy? Yea we pullin out now. Which one? Lenox? Hold on." He took the phone from his ear and looked at me, "You wanna go to Lenox?"

"Yea that's cool" I said nodding.

"Bruh? Yea that's straight. We headed there now. Wait til you see what I'm finna pull up on y'all boys in. You'll see. Yea."

"You putting on today for real ain't you?"
"I told you Miss Lady we celebrating and
we stuntin today. I been so focused on running
my check up that I ain't even stopped to enjoy
it. I cant spend it when I'm gone so
we finna enjoy it now. I done accomplished my
goal now its time to sit back and enjoy the ride."
He said with his chest poked out.
"Look at you over there all proud with
that lil bird chest all poked out!" I said poking
him in the chest.
"Naw ain't nothing bird over here." He said and
poked his chest out even more. We laughed
together.
*Mama he keeps me laughing all the time. I wish
you coulda met him.*
That thought made me sad instantly. I laid my
head back against the seat and fought the
tears. I didn't want to ruin his day.
Not today Corinne. Not today.
Jabari grabbed my hand, interlocking his
fingers with mine, and kissed the back of my
hand.
"You good Miss Lady? She watching over you
from up there and you got me down here. I
know I can't fill that void but I'ma do my best."
Jabari said kissing my hand.
"I'm so sorry baby I was tryna hold it in," I said
through the tears, "I just wish she coulda met
you. How you knew I was thinking about my
mama any way?" I said trying to change the
subject.
"That's the only time you get real quiet and
upset. Corinne for real though, don't ever
apologize to me again about getting upset
bout yo mama. It don't bother me. Matter
fact I'm proud of you cause I don't even know

how to show emotion for my pops or mama. I know your firsts without her gone be hard but I'm here to support you through 'em all and to catch every tear. It's my job."

If I wasn't in love with him before that moment I definitely was now. The fact that I had someone to catch my falling tears gave me strength and the sadness I had at that moment went out the window.

We pulled up to Lenox Square Mall and circled the parking lot looking for his boys. When we spotted them they were all standing outside their cars shooting the breeze. They didn't recognize the car so we were able to pull in the row directly across from them. None of them even looked up.

"Let me see how long it's gone take for these niggas to notice they surroundings." He said in a serious tone.

"What you mean?" I said.

"In these streets you gotta watch your surroundings. If a car pull up around you and don't nobody get out in a reasonable amount of time watch that car. It might be them folks, might be a duck ass nigga that's lurkin. You gotta watch your surroundings Corinne. When you get ya car and you driving by yourself make sure you watch the four cars behind you. If they making all the same turns call me and I'll tell you where to meet me."

I kept my eyes on his patnas tryna guess which one was gone notice first.

"You listening to me Corinne?" I could hear the seriousness in his tone so I gave him my full attention.

Yes Im listening baby."

"I'm not tryna scare you, and I ain't calling you scary, I'm just saying these streets ain't no joke and you can't play with em. Just promise me you'll listen and do what I'm telling you when it come to these streets."

"I promise Jabari."

We were looking at each other and when we looked back at his boys one of them had spotted the car. Bubba had his hand on his waist, Slim and Fatboy were standing by Slim's car with the trunk halfway popped and I didn't see Memphis anywhere.

"Baby let ya boys know it's us....where Memphis at?"

"He behind the car. He the one let em know we wasn't them folks." he said smiling.

Jabari got out the car and yelled, "Yea it took ya'll boys long enough!" They all laughed and walked over to our car dapping each other up. I was watching them when Bubba walked over to my side and opened the door.

"What up Cee why you sittin in the car?
Get yo big head ass out!" He said laughing.

Jabari was right behind him, "She betta not had opened that door while she wit me," he winked at me and I playfully rolled my eyes, "and if you wasn't her cousin we'd have an issue bout you comin over here to open her door!"

"Daaammmnnn Cee what you did wit
my patna and who is this nigga?!?" They laughed and dapped each other up.

"Cee you gottem gone. I ain't never seen
my bruh like this. Opening doors and shit.
Smiling like a damn fat kid wit cake. But hey my cuz deserved it so do ya'll thang." Bubba said looking back and forth between me and Jabari.

Everybody burst out laughing. I got out the car and gave Bubba a hug. I responded to everybody else "What up shawty's" with handshakes. As they were all standing around talking about the new car I noticed a girl walking up. I kept my eyes on her. Once she was closer I recognized her; it was Memphis's baby mama Monica. I met her a couple of times before and I liked her, she was down to earth.

"Hey girl," she greeted with a smile walking over to me, "I'm glad you here I thought I was gone be by myself with these clowns." She looked at them and rolled her eyes jokingly.

"I thought I was too." I replied relieved. I wanted to get Jabari something but there was no way I was gone be able to shake him if I was the only female.

"See y'all niggas out here talkin' and shit ya'll know everything close early today. It's already 2 somethin." Bubba said as he turned and started walking.

"What you in a hurry for nigga?" Fatboy said laughing

"I couldn't decide who I'ma celebrate with tonight so shit I'ma go in this mall and pick up a New Year's broad. Gimme a sec Corinne and Monica I got ya'll a friend coming right up."

"We good" we said in unison.

We all laughed and went in the mall, Monica and I walking together while the guys walked behind us.

"I love this cut on you." I said to Monica, she was sporting a new bob.

"Thank you girl I did it this morning. Something new for the New Year." She said running her hands through it.

You got down on that."

"I love them layers you rocking too and that long ass hair of yours girl! You need to let me silk press it for you." Monica said twirling a strand of my hair.

"I was really thinking about that the other day. We need to set something up."

We made it to the food court and grabbed a table while Bubba and Slim got something to eat. Monica winked at me and initiated our break away conversation.

"Hey fellas the ladies wanna do a lil shopping on our own."

Jabari and Memphis looked at each other and made some kind of silent agreement.

"Aight." They said one after the other.

"Yall give us a sec right quick. We'll be right back." Jabari said as he got up and motioned for me to come with him.

When we were out of ear range I asked where we were going.

"We gotta run back out to the car real quick. I ain't think we was gone separate so I got all the money on me. I ain't gone give you no large amount in here and you finna be walking by yourself. I'ma give it to you in the car."

He was always so careful and I was thankful for it. We got in the car and he asked for my purse. He started transferring bank roll after bank roll from the Louis bag he always kept on him to my Michael Kors.

"That's 15 bands."

"I ain't gone need all that baby!"

"Get whatever you want Miss Lady. Where your pistol?" He asked with a serious tone. He had bought me a .380 and taught me how to shoot it a month after we started talking.

"It's in there you ain't see it?" he moved the money around and looked.

"Yea I see it. I hate you walking around with this amount on you by yourself. I'ma just start putting money on your bank card so you don't have to carry cash. Keep your eyes and ears open Corinne."

"I will."

He ain't playing bout stuntin, 15 bands?

We walked back in the mall and up to the food court. When we got there Monica stood up and said, "You ready girl?"

I kissed Jabari and he whispered, "Eyes and ears."

"Okay baby." I said and we walked off.

"Thank you girl for getting us away. I was trying to figure out how I was gone break away cause I wanna get Jabari something."

"Aww that's sweet and no problem girl I ain't have time for them to be rushin us to pick something out. What you thinking bout getting him?"

"I don't know yet. I know I don't wanna get him clothes though. He buy an outfit and shoes every day I swear. I wanna get him something that says I appreciate you."

Monica looked at me and smiled, "I see why he love you."

"Love me?" I questioned. Today was our first time saying I love you to one another and we were by ourselves.

"Yea, love you. This ain't nothing I done heard him say this something I done observed. When he with you he different. Happier. Worry free. I done been with Memphis for 3 years now and I ain't never seen Jabari like this. It's like y'all the only two people in the world when ya'll together. Ya'll love is one of a kind and you can tell it from the outside looking in. You appreciate him for reasons other than his status in them streets. That's what he need girl. That's what any street nigga need." She explained. What she was saying meant so much to me. It was confirmation of everything he had already told me.

Monica was still talking about our relationships with Jabari and Memphis when I looked up and saw what I was going to get him.

"My bad girl but that's what I'ma get him," I said pointing at a watch on display in the Tourneau window, "....a watch. He don't like to be flashy but he deserve it."

We headed in to the Tourneau store and over to one of the counters.

"Oooh girl look at that one!" Monica said enthusiastically about a gold diamond encrusted one.

"He not a fan of gold but that is hot. I like how it's made."

Our conversation was interrupted by the clearing of a throat. When I looked up to see who it was there was an older white sales woman standing over us.

"How may I help you two?" The way she said *you* made the hairs on my neck stand up. I looked at Monica and back at the lady.

"Well Barbara," I said looking at her name tag, "We are looking for a watch for my significant other. Can you help us with that?"

"Well these are diamond encrusted, gold, platinum, or white gold time pieces ranging in price from 5,000 to 50,000 dollars. If you come over here I can show you our less expensive brands of watches." And she turned to walk away.

My blood was boiling and it took everything in me not to jump over the counter and beat the hell out of the sales woman.

Breath. You'll go to jail and she ain't worth it.

"Oh hell naw! Come on Corinne 'fore we end up in jail!" Monica said ready at any moment to spaz on Barbara.

I clenched my teeth and turned to Monica, "Naw we finna cash out on this broad."

"Excuse me Barbara but do you have a manager I can speak with?" I asked in a professional tone.

She turned around with a confused look. "Is there something I can help you with?"

"Barbara I need you to go get your manager. We are done speaking with you."

Her cheeks became flush and she walked off flipping her hair to go get her or him. When she returned she had a dark haired, foreign gentleman with her. His accent was heavy.

"How may I help you ladies?

Stay calm Corinne.

"Hello Hussein," I said reaching out my hand to shake his, "I usually have a pleasant experience when I come here but today isn't going so well."

He looked over at Barbara then back at me.

"I apologize for that Ms.......?" He said fishing for my name.

"Jackson. Corinne Jackson."

"Ms. Jackson what might the problem be?"

I looked at Barbara and smiled, "My sister and I came in looking for a watch for my significant other. When we looked in this particular case we were approached by Barbara and told how expensive these watches were and referred to another case as if I didn't have the money for a watch from this case. I personally am really offended and have never been treated with such disrespect. My family has been customers of this store for a couple of years now and I just wanted to let you know about the poor customer service before I report this incident to the Better Business Bureau and take our business elsewhere." I was putting on the show of a lifetime.

Hussein looked at Barbara again with a clenched jaw then turned to us with a look of concern.

"I offer my sincerest apologies for any trouble you were given here today. Please allow me to assist you myself; we don't want to lose you or your family as customers. And I assure you this matter will be handled by me directly and it will not be taken lightly. Barbara you owe these young ladies an apology."

She was fire engine red as she walked up to us. "I apologize for offending you ladies."

"Now please wait for me in my office." Hussein said to her as she turned to walk away. She looked at him then at us. I winked.

Bet she won't she try nobody else. Racist ass.

"Now what can I help you ladies with? You said a watch for your significant other? Did you like something in this case in particular?" He was sweating bullets behind my threats.

I looked at Monica and smirked; she was all smiles.

"Yes I like the style of this one here but I don't like it in gold. Does it come in something else?" Oh yes that's a fine choice and it comes in Gold, White Gold, or Platinum."

"Can I see it in White Gold?"

He bent down and grabbed the white gold version of the watch Monica had picked out from under the glass case. "This is a Breitling, one of our signature time pieces. The dial is fully encrusted with diamonds...totaling in at 2 and a half carats and It has a stainless steel casing. This is a wonderful time piece Ms. Jackson."

"I really like this. How much am I looking at?"

He looked at the tag. "This piece is 20,000 dollars but right now it's on sale for 16.5."

I didn't break a sweat. "And what about the warranty?"

"It comes with a lifetime warranty and lifetime diamond replacement. And of course because of your trouble today I will throw in my discount of Fifty percent off bringing your total to 8,250." He said with his chest poked out like he had just done the best thing of his life.

"What you think girl? Think he'll like it?"

"Like it? I think he gone love it. He better marry you and I ain't playing!" She said laughing.

I turned to Hussein and smiled. "I'll take it."

It was like a sigh of relief had come over him and he showed it in his smile. "Well, let us ring you up and I'll get your warranty paper work ready. Come this way Ms. Jackson."

We walked to the cash register and finalized the order.

"How will you be paying for this today Ms. Jackson?"

"Cash." I said proudly.

Hussein tried to hide his shock and Monica was smiling super hard.

"Give me a second please." And he walked back towards his office.

When Hussein returned he had Barbara with him.

"Barbara please ring up Ms. Jackson I already entered in all her information." He said and I swore I saw him smirk.

Her face was red with embarrassment and anger. "Your total is 8,745 dollars."

I politely opened my purse and placed nine stacks on the counter in a neat pile. Barbara's eyes widened as she looked at the cash on the counter. She grabbed each stack one after the other removing the rubber band. It took her ten minutes to count the money.

"Your change is 255 dollars." She said dryly as she counted the money back to me.

"Thank you for shopping with us today ladies," Hussein said handing me Jabari's present, "Please come back and see us soon." Hussein said with a smile.

"We'll be back thank you for your help." I turned to Barbara. "Thank you too Ms. Barbara. Have you a blessed rest of the day." We walked out of the store smiling ear to ear.

We spent the rest of our time shopping and talking about Barbara, her judgment and the look on her face when I put the stacks on the counter.

"Her face was priceless I should have took a picture! And was that story about your family always shopping there true?" Monica asked killing herself with laughter.

"Naw girl I ain't never been in that store but I had to make Barbara pay for that."

"You definitely did that!"

We made our way in to BeBe where I was able to find a dress and some heels for the evening, then on to Macy's for sexy bra and panty sets and we ended the shopping trip in Ralph Lauren. When we were finished shopping we met the guys back in the food court. They all had bags of their own and were deep in conversation when we walked up. Jabari spotted us first tapping Memphis to let him know of our presence.

"You got everything you wanted Miss Lady?" he asked greeting me with a kiss.

"Yes and then some." I responded eager to show him his gift.

Wait till ya'll alone.

Jabari looked back at his boys, "Ya'll ready? Everybody got up and started heading to the exit. We were turning heads left and right with all the bags we all had. Everybody had done a little shopping spree of their own. When we got to the parking lot Monica and I grabbed the keys and walked ahead to our car while the guys stood around making plans for later on that evening.

"He gone love that watch girl and that dress. You got down with that."

"Thank you love! Memphis gone love everything you got too. I'm really glad you came."

"Ok let me get to this car these bags heavy. I'll see you later on tonight. You want me to do your make up?"

"You know I don't wear nothing but lip gloss." I laughed

"Well tonight we gone give you some lashes and some eye shawdow. What you doing with ya hair?" She asked.

"I'ma put it up in a high bun." I said demonstrating with my hands.

"Oh that's gone be cute. Okay I'll see you later on. Ain't no telling what we finna do now."

"Okay, see you later." We exchanged hugs and Monica walked to their car.

I sat the bags on the backseat of the Benz and got in. I watched as the fellas had what looked to be a group meeting. Jabari was doing the talking while the rest of the guys were soaking up everything he was saying. His demeanor was so powerful but without the arrogance.

Mama I love him so much. I hope you love him too. I think tonight is the night and I'm so nervous. He's my husband though Mama I know it.

I was so caught up in my thoughts that I didn't even see the meeting end or Jabari walking to the car. When he opened the door I was startled.

"You straight? I ain't scare you did I?" He was laughing.

"Naw." I replied sarcastically.

We pulled out the Parking lot heading towards the highway.

"You can put on whatever you wanna listen to Miss Lady."

I smiled as I reached in the middle console and grabbed T.I's paper Trail album. I put it on and went straight to "Whatever You Like".

Jabari smirked and turned the radio up. I closed my eyes, relaxed in my seat and drifted off into an unexpected sleep.

Chapter 7: Corinne

When I finally opened my eyes again we were
downtown pulling into The W, one of Atlanta's
finest hotels.

"Welcome back." Jabari said with a smile.

"My bad baby I ain't even know I was sleep. We
at The W?" a smile spread across my face.

Jabari grabbed all the bags and we got out
valet. To my surprise Memphis and Monica did
too.

"Oh my gosh did you know about this Corinne?"
Monica said showing her surprise.

"Nope. I'm just as surprised as you."

We walked in the hotel and were instructed to
wait while Memphis and Jabari went over to the
counter. I recognized the girl they were checking
in with as Memphis's sister Monique. She
waved and we returned the gesture. After a

couple of minutes we headed up to the Extremely Wow suite. I was blown away by the beauty of the room. It had two bedrooms, a dining room, ceiling to floor windows overlooking the city, a huge bar and walk-in showers that a small group could fit in. I could feel Jabari watching my every move; loving my reaction. I could hear Monica calling my name from the Master room,

"Corinne girl look!"

I hurried into the Master bathroom and saw an amazing vanity and massage chairs set up. My eyes widened with excitement.

"Definitely getting me a massage!"

We gave each other high fives and walked back into the living room of the suite where Memphis was already hitting up the bar.

"Shots for everybody!" Memphis yelled looking for glasses.

I walked over to Jabari and gave him a kiss and a hug.

"Thank you so much baby for spoiling me, for loving me, for everything you do for me and for everybody else. Thank you for just being you." I said looking in his eyes.

He wrapped his arms around me and pulled me close to him, "You the best thing ever happen to me Corinne. I love you." Then he kissed me.

"Aye love birds come take ya'll shots." Monica said calling us over to the bar.

We walked over and grabbed one of the four shot glasses of 1800.

Memphis held up his shot, "A toast to wealth in this new year."

Monica held hers up, "A toast to health."

"A toast to loyalty and royalties." Jabari said lifting his glass.

"A toast to love." I said raising mine.

We all toasted our glasses and threw the shots back. The 1800 burned going down but I tried my best to keep a straight face.

"What time it is bruh?" Jabari asked Memphis.

"5:36." He responded looking at his phone.

"Aight bruh we finna go chill in the room. Bubba nem said they gone pull up bout 9. So I guess we gone pull out bout 10."

"Aight, how you getting ya chevy?" Memphis asked.

"Fatboy ridin wit Slim tonight so he gone pick it up from the garage and drive it down here."

"Bet. I'm bout to po' up and chill myself." Memphis said as they dapped up.

We grabbed our shopping bags and overnight bags and took them in the Master room. Jabari closed and locked the door behind him as I laid across the king size bed sinking in to the pillow top mattress.

"Oh my God baby this bed is so soft."

He laughed and came and laid beside me.

"Oh yea we getting one of these Miss Lady." He said closing his eyes.

Give it to him now.

"I got something for you Jabari." I said with excitement building in my stomach.

"What's is it?"

I got up and grabbed the Tourneau bag and handed it to him.

"I got you this just to let you know I appreciate you."

He had a look of astonishment on his face as he opened the box. He looked at me then at the watch then at me again.

"Corinne you got this for me? *For me?* Man ain't nobody but my grandmamma ever got me a gift. And ain't nobody ever got me nothing like this. Shawty this shit mean something to me for real." He pulled me off the bed and hugged me tight. "Corinne how much you spent on this? I saw this watch in gold the other day when I was in there and the man wanted 20 bands for it."

"I spent a little less than half of that but the exact amount don't matter. You deserve it baby."

"Amounts won't ever matter for us if I can help it but what I'm saying is you had to spend at least 12 bands and I only gave you 15. Corinne instead of spending the 15 on yourself you bought something for me? Shawty you don't understand what that mean to me." He closed the box to the watch and placed it on the dresser then walked back over to me. We stood there looking in each other's eyes for a couple of minutes. I was shaking from nerves then he wrapped his arms around me and the nerves went away.

"I love you Corinne. I ain't never loved like I love you. Are you sure you ready cause I'll wait for you as long as I have to."

I don't know if it was how he said it or what he said but he had me falling in love with him all over again.

"You're the only person to ever make me fall in love with them daily. I'm sure Jabari. I'm ready."

I had never been this nervous in my life. I didn't know what to expect or what to do. He must have sensed my nervousness by the way my hands were shaking.

"Calm down Corinne. I got you."

Jabari moved our bags off the bed and pulled the covers back while I stood there watching his every move. My thoughts were racing.

This is really about to happen. Breath. Calm down. I hope it don't hurt bad. I don't know what to do!

By now it was dark outside and with all the lights off in the room the city night life shined bright. It was beautiful. Jabari saw me looking towards the window and went and opened the curtains. The lights from the city below shined bright illuminating his silhouette. He took his shirt off and walked towards me. My heart skipped a beat. He grabbed my hands and led me to the bed, sitting down in front of me on the edge of the mattress. He kissed my stomach through my shirt then lifted it to take it off. I helped him and let it drop to the floor.

Whew! I'm so glad I chose this panty set.

Jabari ran his hands down my stomach and then around to unfasten my bra.

"Yo' skin so soft Miss Lady."

I couldn't speak. I just watched his every move and assisted where I could.

My bra fell to the floor and Jabari kissed both of my nipples. The sensation sent chills all over my body. He stood and laid me down on the bed kissing my neck and down my stomach. When he got to my jeans he unbuttoned them and slid them along with my panties over my hips and onto the floor. Jabari stood back and admired my shape. In that moment I was so glad I had a habit of shaving my entire body every day. He got down on his knees and pulled me by my waist to the end of the bed placing my legs on his shoulders. I had imagined what this would be like many times before but no imaginative thought could have prepared my body for the feeling his tongue gave my womanhood. The spine tingling sensation kept my back arched and the juices flowing. When he was done there Jabari removed the rest of his clothes and got in the bed with me pulling the covers halfway over our bodies. He kissed me all over calming my nerves with every touch of his lips. When I stopped shaking Jabari grabbed the condom he had placed beside me and put it on. "You ready?" he whispered in my ear.

"Yes." I responded breathing heavily.

At that moment Jabari took a part of me that no man ever had. He entered me slowly and gently kissing me every step of the way. The pain was excruciating at first but the passion that we shared in that moment overpowered what I was feeling. The love that evolved between us took us both to another place and to climax after climax. Jabari made love to me for another hour or so before we both passed out. He held me tight and kissed the back of my neck. The last words I remembered hearing were, "You my wife Corinne." Then we both drifted off into a peaceful sleep.

Chapter 8: Jabari

Bzzzz. Bzzzz. Bzzzz.

My phone woke me up.

"What up?"

"Ya'll up bruh?" Memphis asked.

I looked at my screen. 8:58 pm.

"We finna get up now. Bubba nem here?"

"They said they finna pull up. Slim had to catch a bite."

"Aight bet. We up."

"Bet."

Click.

I kissed the back of Corinne's neck and she stirred just a little. She smelled so good even after sweating. I was her first and I definitely was gone be her last. I had taken a couple of virginities when I was younger but none in the last couple of years. I had forgotten what the sensation was like and the one Corinne gave me was every bit of amazing. Even if I had to put in all the work until she found her own rhythm it was worth it. Not only was Corinne beautiful inside and definitely out, sex with her had me mesmerized. I wanted her to be mine forever. Nobody's opinion mattered. I didn't care who thought what or how long we had been together I was going to wife her up literally.

I got up and put my boxers on and turned on the lights to the room and bathroom.

Corinne didn't budge. I walked over to the bed and sat beside her. She was beautiful when she slept.

"Miss Lady." I said kissing her ear.

She opened her eyes and smiled.

"Yes baby?" I loved hearing her say that.

"We gotta get dressed. Bubba nem finna pull up and I told everybody we was pulling out round 10."

She stretched then sat up pulling the sheets up around her chest. Her hair fell around her face and onto her shoulders.

"It's kinda cold in here can you turn on the heat for a sec?"

"Yea I got you. How you feel?" I asked walking to the heater.

She looked at me for a second like she was trying to find the right words.

"Physically I'm sore," She gave me a sexy smirk, "...but emotionally.....I've never felt a love like this." I loved how open she was with me.

A couple of minutes later, once the room had heated up, she got up and headed for the shower. I watched her naked body as she walked. She didn't have any blemishes on her silky smooth skin.

Damn I wanna feel her again.

Once I heard the water cut on I went into the bathroom. We had never showered together but there was a first time for everything and I wanted to get in.

"Can I get in wit you?"

She slid the glass shower door open and peeped her head out.

"Please." She said in an inviting tone.

I knew my niggas was out there ready to party but I was lost in Corinne at the moment. They was gone have to wait.

I climbed in the shower and walked up behind Corinne putting my hands on her waist. Nothing turned me on more than to see the water running down her body. She turned, faced me and laid her head on my chest. I ran my hands down her back. Even under the water her skin was silky smooth. I couldn't resist. I picked her up putting her back against the shower wall and entered her slowly. No matter how excited she made me I kept in mind she said she was sore. Her breathing became a shallow pant and she wrapped her arms and legs around me.

"Ja-Jabari what about the condom?" she managed to get out in between strokes.

"You mine Corinne. It's me and you from here on out. I want you to be my wife and the mother of my kids." I was tryna keep my mind clear so I could prolong the moment but the mixture of water, Corinne's juices, and her soft skin had other plans. I released inside her and didn't even hesitate or try to stop it. All the rules I had lived by when it came to love and females was out the window when It came to Corinne. Grandmama always told me when I found that one she would change me from the inside out. She knew Corinne was the one the first time she met her. I remember her telling me when we went for Thanksgiving that I had some choices to make either the streets or Corinne cause she was my wife. I asked her how she knew and she smiled and said, "Cause baby she's the one I prayed for." From that moment Corinne did nothing but make what my grandma said clearer and clearer.

We washed our spontaneous passion off and got out the shower. I checked my phone. 9:48. I had a couple missed calls and a text from Memphis letting me know Bubba, Slim, and Fatboy had pulled up.

"They out there waiting on us baby. You can take your time and handle what you gotta handle. I'ma get dressed and head out there with them. She nodded in approval and continued drying her hair. I walked over to her and kissed her forehead. "You and my grandmamma ain't gone want for nothing and that's on my pops."

She just smiled and kissed me on the lips. I could look in her face and see she was in deep thought. When she got like that I left her to herself. I knew she was either thinking bout her mama or about no longer being a virgin. If I needed to catch her tears I would but this look wasn't one of sadness. It was more of a pondering look.

"You good right Miss Lady?" I said making sure.

"Yes baby I'm good."

I walked in the room and grabbed my clothes. It was a Polo type of night. I picked up a black and Grey Polo outfit at the mall earlier and some smoke grey Polo boots. As I got dressed I glanced in the bathroom and got lost watching

Corinne lotion her body. She was so damn sexy. I had to turn my back to the door to keep from going back in the bathroom for round 3. I looked in the mirror and checked the fit then threw on some Ralph Lauren cologne. I picked up the box from Tourneau and grabbed the watch out.

Damn I can't believe she got me this watch.

I couldn't remember the last time I had gotten a gift from somebody other than my Grandmama. The fact that Corinne used the lil money I gave her to buy something for me spoke volumes. Shawty was the truth; a total package and she continued to show me why she deserved the world. I couldn't stop smiling and the way the light was hitting the watch shit I couldn't stop shining either. I never had been a flashy nigga, it brought too much attention, but the way this watch was hitting it was time to build my jewelry game up. Corinne walked out the bathroom and caught me flexed up in the mirror. She laughed so hard.

"Glad to know you like it!" She said through the laughter.

I couldn't even put on like I didn't. There was rumors about me sitting on weight but nobody but the dope boys I supplied knew for sure. Now I had a 20,000 dollar watch on my wrist; wasn't no hiding it.

"Yea I really appreciate this. Aight I'm headed out here you want me to send Monica in here to do ya'll lil makeup thang?"

"Boy get outta here..Make up thang?" she laughed, "Yea tell her to come here please."

I walked out the room ready for my niggas to clown me for taking so long. It was 10:18 but

we wasn't in no rush; long as we was in the
club to say Happy New Year's.

"Bout time ol pretty ass boy!" Bubba yelled
before I could get out the room door good. He
was at the bar rolling a blunt. Slim
and Fatboy were chillin on the couches and
Memphis and Monica were looking out the
window over the city.

"What up yall? My bad. My bad." I dapped
everybody up with my left hand making sure
they could see me shining.

"Ok ok! I see you bruh!" Fatboy was the first to
say something bringing everybody over to see
the hype.

"Damn bruh that shit fi. When you cop that?"
Bubba asked in between sealing his blunt.

"My girl got it for me today." I said sliding my
shirt up my wrist so they could get a better
glimpse. The attention wasn't thirsty cause all
of us had a check but they definitely wasn't use
to seeing me be flashy. They knew how I felt
about that.

"Damn bruh that's a Breitling." Memphis said
walking up closer for a better look. He was the
jewelry expert and was always copping
something new.

"Oh Monica my bad Corinne told me to ask you
to come here."

"Ok. My girl got down on that though. You
better marry her." She was a little tipsy already
but I knew she was dead serious; she said it all
the time.

When I looked back at my niggas Slim was over
by the window on the phone.

He probably juggin'.

"Shawty love yo ass. That's bout 15, 20 bands
on ya wrist." Memphis said while dapping me

up and bringing my attention back to the watch. "That's the move. When ya'll getting married?" he said joking.

"Shit why you playing I'ma marry shawty for real." That statement caught Bubba attention. He looked me in my eye and pulled his blunt. "You love Cee for real don't you?" He asked staring at me eye to eye.

I turned and faced him head on. The room got quiet and everybody came and stood round us. We all knew how he felt about Corinne and I knew he was gone ask me man to man about her sooner or later. Since she didn't have a father to give her away I respected his over protectiveness.

"Real talk, shawty the best thang every happen to me and her loyalty run deep. When them streets got a nigga nerves bad Corinne the only one that keep me focused. She a different breed from every broad I know. She ain't about how she can come up; she about how we can come up and I love her for that." I explained.

"You my nigga and I'ma ride wit you through whatever. You know that. But Corinne my blood and she more than just my lil cuz....that's my lil suh. I need you to give me your word bruh that you got her. No matter what's going on in these streets you got her." I couldn't do nothing but respect where he was coming from these streets was hell.

Slim, Fatboy and Memphis were passing a blunt between each other waiting for me to respond.

"Bruh I got her. In every way possible I got her." We stood looking at each other for a couple of seconds then Bubba spoke.

"Well shit now you my brother for real!" Bubba said and dapped me up. I knew I needed

Bubba's blessing and I had it. Corinne loved me but I didn't think she would go against Bubba.
"Congrats my nigga" Fatboy said
"My nigga bout to be a married man! Congrats bruh." Memphis threw in. Slim came over and gave me dap, "That's what's up bruh." Something in his voice wasn't right.
What up with this nigga? Naw he probably high as hell.
Fatboy broke up my thoughts, "Shit when the wedding and I know I'm the best man."
"Boy watch out! I got that!" Memphis argued. I just laughed and watched them go back and forth.
"Aye ya'll she don't know nothing. I ain't decided how I'ma do it yet." I said motioning for them to quiet down.
And as if on que the room door opened and Corinne and Monica walked out. I couldn't take my eyes off her. Fatboy tapped me on the back and whispered, "Yea bruh gone head and wife her up."
I smiled. She was bad as hell. Corinne had her hair pulled up in a bun that complimented her beauty. Her Royal blue Bebe dress hugged every curve she had showing off how small her waist and flat her stomach was. Her legs were oiled up and silky smooth standing firm in her diamond studded, gold accented heels. Plus her jewelry matched her shoes. I was choosin and I knew my patnas was too but they knew not to let me see it. I loved the fact that my girl could turn heads just not my patnas heads.
"Hey ya'll." Corinne spoke and waved to everybody. Monica walked out behind her with her chest poked out proud of her finished product.

"Yea I got ya girl make up flawless." She said
smiling.
Corinne walked over to me, "My bad for taking
so long."
"You good Miss Lady no need to apologize. You
look beautiful by the way and that
dress Mmm Mmm Mmm."
"Thank you baby."
"Ohhh Ohhhh Ya big head ass don't see nobody
else." Bubba said walking over to us.
She smiled real big and gave him a hug, "Shut
up boy you know I was coming to give you some
love! You look nice uh oh I see you" she said
joking with Bubba.
"I see you too and it look like you gone
have Jabari shootin up the whole damn club."
Everybody laughed.
I looked at my phone. 10:40.
"Ya'll ready to pull?" I asked
Everybody threw in their yea's and we all
headed out the door. When we got to the Lobby
all eyes was on us. Valet brought the cars
around and we could see people around the
hotel looking to see if we were celebrities. We
were in the Chevy's for the night. I had a Royal
Blue 69' Chevelle with black racing stripes and
black leather interior that coincidently matched
Corinne's dress to a tee. Memphis had a orange
'72 Chevelle SS with white interior and some
Rally's. Slim and Fatboy was in Slim's black on
black 1970 Nova and Bubba followed up with
the canary yellow '68 Camaro with white leather
interior. All of us had candied paint jobs.
We had quite a crowd gathered outside, you
couldn't tell us nothing. I put in Jeezy's The
Recession album and turned up "Put On". I
could hear them revving their engines behind

me. We was gone show out in the city tonight. I had my girl on my right, my niggas behind me, and I was sitting on a check. Life couldn't get any better.

Chapter 9: Corinne

It was the Friday of Valentine's Day weekend and I was excited to see what Jabari had planned for me. He had been nothing short of sweet since New Year's weekend; reassuring me that I was more to him than just the sex we couldn't seem to keep ourselves away from. We were each other's backbones and the love making was a plus. I was beginning to get my own rhythm and Jabari couldn't resist. He taught me how he liked to be pleased and I mastered each lesson. I didn't want for anything so in return I made sure he had a hot meal every night and a passionate night cap. I was head over heels in love with him and did whatever I had to do to make sure he was happy.
I picked up the phone and called him.
"Hey my love."

"What up Miss Lady."

How's it coming along?" I asked. He had rented a house on the South Side off of Flat Shoals two weeks before and was having it turned into a studio. It was a lucrative business venture because everybody these days wanted to be a rapper.

"Oh it's coming along good. They just finished putting in the glass to the booth and installing all the cabling and me, Yoshi and Dough putting the tables up." Yoshi and Dough were his patnas that ran the trap houses on the South Side.

"Oh they there with you...that's good."

"Yea you know they'll be holding this down on a daily." I knew he meant as security but I didn't ask no questions.

"Oh Ok. When is the other equipment gone be here?" I asked.

"The mixer, speakers and mics should be here tomorrow along with the couches and stuff you picked out."

"Yea cause all three of the Macs came today." I informed him. We were still in the process of searching for a home for us to share so all the studio equipment was shipped to my house.

"Oh okay well shit we should be up and running in the next week or so and I'll let you handle the decorating sometime next week."

I laughed, "Them folks ain't gone care about no decorations baby. They gone be high or focused on recording."

"Gotta keep a professional appearance for these niggas though cause the prices gone be real professional," he laughed, "I got top of the line equipment coming in here."

"You crazy boy. Well I just called to check on you and tell you I love you and of course to remind you not to be late." I had a romantic dinner planned for him and I needed everything to go as planned.

"You know I ain't forgot that Miss Lady. Eight at our spot right?" We had been going to The W every weekend and I loved the suites and the memories we were making there.

"Yes baby."

"Ok I'll be heading that way after I pick up the mail." When he said that it meant it was time for him to pick up his money from his trap houses.

"I need to bring something?" he asked.

"Just an appetite and my wood." I answered seductively.

"Damn girl.....I'ma be there 10 minutes early." We both laughed.

"Ok see you in a little while. I'm heading over there now. I love you Jabari." I said.

"I love you too and drive safe Corinne." I had been driving the Mercedes since New Year's and he was always nervous about me not paying attention to my surroundings.

"Ok."

Don't forget to text me what room."

"Ok baby."

"Yea."

Click.

I was excited about the night I had planned out. We were going to have a candlelit dinner from Ruth's Chris Steak House followed by a rose petal bath, then the performance of a routine I had been working on for two weeks. I always had a natural talent to dance but I wanted to do some tricks on the pole for my man and had been sneaking to take pole dancing classes since the middle of January preparing for this night. I looked at the time. It was 6:02. I knew Jabari wouldn't be late; he hated to keep me waiting, so I grabbed the keys and headed out the door.

The car had been packed since I got off work at 3:00. Jabari hated that I still kept my job. He felt like it made him look like less of a man because he had a check and I worked. He felt like he wasn't taking care of home or something. He never pressed the issue long; just let me know how he felt then he would leave it alone. Mama had always said, "Hold your own Corinne. Don't let a man do everything for you unless he your husband cause if it fall through you gone be the one S.O.L." I knew he loved me but I was holding on to Mama's advice.

I headed downtown fighting through I-75 traffic and grabbed our food, reaching the hotel at 6:53.

Ok Corinne you got an hour to get everything set up.

I let valet park the car and I picked up the room keys from the front desk. Thoughts from New Year's flooded my memory as I made my way to our suite. It was *that* night I realized just how good Jabari's face card was. When we pulled up to the club the line was wrapped around the building. We walked right up to the door, Jabari dapped up security and we walked straight in. The DJ shouted him and his boys out over the loud speaker as we walked through the club and up to the overlooking VIP section. We was too turnt up that night popping bottles and blowing hella gas. And even though we

were in a club full of people Jabari still
managed to make me feel like the only woman
standing. When it was time to count down he
kissed me and we brought in the New Year's in
our own little world. I smiled to myself when my
thoughts were interrupted by my phone ringing.
"Hey baby."
"What up Corinne you made it?" he asked
concerned.
"Yes I'm walking to the room now. 304. My bad
baby." I said in an apologetic tone. I forgot to
text him the room number and let him know I
made it safe. He was always so paranoid.
"Aight. We pickin up this last lil bit of mail and
then I'm headed that way." I could hear in his
tone he was frustrated. I didn't know if it was
because I didn't call or something else but I
knew I couldn't ask him over the phone.
"Okay baby I'm here."
We got off the phone and I headed into the
room. I had requested that room service heat up
our food in the hotel kitchen, transfer it onto
plates and deliver it back to me by 7:45. Of
course I had to slide an extra tip to the bell hop
and the cook. Before the bell hop left I asked
him to help me move the dining table for two
over to by the windows. We were going to
overlook the city while we ate.
After I was alone, I began setting up the
candles I had bought placing them all around
the suite. I was waiting till the food came to
light them. After I set up almost 75 tea light
candles I went to the bedroom to set up my 10
ft. travel pole. I set up the pink spotlight I
bought to shine on the pole while I danced and
moved one of the chairs from the living space
into the bedroom for him to sit. He loved going

to the strip club so tonight and every night after I was going to be his own personal stripper.

I checked the time. 7:28.

I went into the bathroom and dumped yellow and red rose petals in the tub. I would run the bath water when we finished eating. The more I set up the more excited I got. I loved to love him.

There was a knock at the door. When I answered I was met by the bell hop bringing our food; 7:45 on the dot. I sat up the table putting some of the leftover rose petals around our plates. I opened the brand new bottle of Crown Royal I got him and filled his glass then opened my bottle of Pink Moscato and poured myself up. I knew he would be there in a couple of minutes so I turned the radio to Kiss 104.1 and began lighting the candles. I made it to the last couple of candles in the bedroom when I heard another knock on the door. I ran to my bag and sprayed a refreshing mist of perfume then went to the door. When I opened it Jabari was standing there with a bouquet of pink roses. I smiled and hugged him tight.

"You look good Miss Lady." And he kissed me.

"Thank you my love." I said and led him to the table pulling his chair out for a change.

"I see you. You got the ol'school and the candles going." He said hitting my butt as I went by. I sat down and grabbed Jabari's hand so we could pray over the food. He squeezed mine and told me he loved me. I looked him in his eyes to tell him I loved him back but something was there. Behind his smile and behind his gaze was a look I hadn't seen on him before.

"I love you too. What's wrong baby?"

He tried to soften his gaze but I saw right through it. "Nothing baby. I'm good. Why you ask that?"

"Intuition." I said with a concerned look.

He rubbed my hands, "You don't miss nothing do you? It ain't nothing I'ma let ruin your Valentine's Day I promise you that but we'll talk about that later. I just wanna enjoy what you done planned for me."

The hairs on the back of my neck stood up. It had to be something in the streets but I wasn't gone press the issue. When he was ready I would be there to listen.

"Okay baby whenever you ready I'm listening."

"I know." And he threw me the familiar smile I was use to.

"That's Crown in your cup. Take a sip and ease ya mind baby." TLC's *Red Light Special* was playing in the background.

"You tryna get me drunk and take advantage of me ain't you?" He asked smiling.

"I definitely am." I said winking at him. I was on my second glass of Moscoto and I was feeling good.

We enjoyed our meal and let the alcohol take its effect. Once we were finished eating I led Jabari to the candlelit bedroom and sat him on the bed. I walked in the bathroom and turned on the water making sure the temperature was just right. When I walked back into the room Jabari was smiling from ear to ear.

"What this stripper pole doing in here?" He had an idea I could dance but he had never really just seen me in action. Tonight that was going to change.

"Be patient baby." I said kissing and nibbling on his ear.

I started taking off his clothes one by one and then I took off mine. I grabbed him by the hand and led him into the bathroom. I turned off the water and stepped in the petal filled tub then pulled him in after me. I sat him down and then sat down behind him grabbing our sponges off of the tub knobs. He leaned back into my chest and I massaged his neck and shoulders. I didn't know what was bothering him but I was gone do whatever to keep his mind off of it. After we had soaked for almost 30 minutes, along with kissing and touching, I soaped up his sponge and washed his body from head to toe then mine. We got out the tub and made our way to the shower to rinse off then I sent him to the room to wait for me. Once he was out of the bathroom I lotioned up real good and changed into a pink lace sheer top and the matching g-string. I put on some 5 inch heels and made my way to the bedroom. Jabari was already sitting in the chair facing pole. His eyes bucked when he saw me, "Damn Miss Lady! I like that...yea I like that." He said licking his lips. I loved the look in his eyes when I turned him on.

I walked over to little boom box I brought to the room and put on Nasty Song by Lil Ru. I climbed the pole and began my routine. I completed every trick I had learned with perfection. Jabari was amazed. He got up and started throwing 100's and 20's tucking them when he could. When Nasty Song went off T.I's *Tip Drill* came on and we had fun with that one. It didn't take much longer for Jabari to want to take the action to the bed. He started the dance mix that was playing over and we moved to the beat; round after round and climax after climax. He no longer had that look from the dinner table in his eyes. Mission accomplished. After about two hours we showered again and then passed out in each other's arms.

I woke up the next morning to Jabari's kisses on my neck. I smiled and when I opened my eyes I was surprised to see him fully dressed.
"Good morning baby. What time is it?" I asked looking for my phone in the sheets.
"Good morning." He said kissing me, "Happy Valentine's Day. Your phone on the night stand and it's 9:45." He said looking at his phone.
"How long you been up?" I asked
"Since 'bout 7. I had to take care of some stuff," he winked, "and then I went and got us some Waffle House."
My stomach growled; I loved their hash browns and blueberry waffles. Jabari brought my plate over to me and sat beside me.
"After you eat get dressed we got some thangs to do." He was smiling.
"Okay and thank you for breakfast."
"After the work you put in last night Miss Lady I knew you was gone wake up hungry." He joked.
"You did ya thang on that pole...where you learned that at?" he asked with one eyebrow raised.
I laughed, "I been taking pole dancing classes since January so I could show out for you last night."
"Oh aight...aight. So I got my own personal stripper?" he was grinning.
"Yes Jabari." I said in between bites.

"Well you made a good lil check last night." He said pointing his head at the nightstand. I looked behind me and my phone was sitting on a stack of bills. I put my fork down and counted the money.

"Seven thousand dollars Jabari?" I said smiling, "This the kinda money you throw in the strip club?"

"Naw they get 5's and 10's...you got 20's and 100's."

We continued talking about the night before while I finished eating. Our conversations flowed so easily that one minute they could be deep and the next it could be just as silly.

I finished eating, got up jumped in the shower again and got dressed. I put on a pink and white Adidas outfit and threw on a brand new pair of pink and white Adidas. Instead of blow drying my hair straight I wore it wet and curly and put on a pink head band to keep the hair out of my face. I looked in the mirror and smiled. I was looking good, smelling good, and I was happy.

Mama I'm so happy. I miss you so much and that won't ever go away but when I'm with him I forget the pain of losing you. I love him Mama. I love him so much.

When I came out the bathroom Jabari was no longer in the room, so I grabbed my purse and headed to the living room of the suite. What I saw brought tears to my eyes. It was like a scene from Case's Happily Ever After video. Jabari was standing in the middle of the room surrounded by hundreds of red and yellow roses. All I could do was put my hand over my face. He walked over to me and led me to the middle of the room by one hand.

"You deserved more than just a dozen so I bought the whole shop." He was grinning again.
"You amazing Jabari and I love you more than words can explain." I kissed him and hugged him tight.
"Baby how we gone get all these outta here?" I said looking around the room at all the roses.
"I'll worry about that when the time comes. You ready?"
"Yea I'm on your time my love." I said smiling.
We headed out the door and down to valet to get the car when Jabari's phone rang.
"What up bruh?" he said listening to caller on the other end. I couldn't hear what the person was saying but I could hear the urgency in their voice. Something was wrong I could feel it but I showed no fear. He would need me to be his strength if things in the streets got too crazy. I watched him intently as his facial expression changed and his jaws tightened. I could feel his body tense up. He wasn't speaking but that look from the other night was back in his eyes.
We got in the car and Jabari ended his call. He was in deep thought as we hopped on I-75 North.
"You okay Jabari?" I asked looking at him and pulling him out of his thoughts.
He grabbed my hand and sucked his teeth. He did that when he was taking his time thinking of what he had to say.
"This your day and I ain't gone let nothing ruin it but I gotta make a change in the plans though. I'ma have to leave you for a couple hours Corinne but I'm sending you to the spa in that time frame. I want you to get whatever you want done and when you finished meet me back at the room. Memphis sending Monica too so

you want be alone. We gone take his car
and I'ma leave our car with you." He looked over
at me watching my expression but I didn't have
one. I was in deep thought now. He always told
me that we wouldn't have any secrets between
us but I knew he wasn't ready to let me in on
what was going on. I paused for a moment
choosing my words carefully.

"That's fine Jabari I ain't never been to the spa.
Thank you." I gave him a smile and rubbed his
leg, "I do need to ask you something though." I
said looking out the window. He had gotten off
on Northside Drive and was now pulling into
the Spa Sydell at Buckhead Plaza. I looked back
at him.

"What's that?" he asked meeting my eyes with
his.

"First I want to let you know that you don't have
to worry about ruining my day baby cause you
make everyday I'm with you feel like Valentine's
Day," That put a smile on his face, "I do know
something wrong though but I understand
you ain't ready to tell me about it." I grabbed
his hand and looked him dead in the eye for the
next part, "Handle what you have to handle
Jabari. Do what you gotta do to protect us and
keep us straight but you come back to me.
Okay?" He nodded in agreement, "No Jabari. I
need to hear you say it. Promise me you'll
always come back to me no matter what happen
in them streets." I didn't crack a smile; I
couldn't have been more serious. I couldn't even
begin to imagine taking another loss and the
thought of it had me on edge. He leaned over
and kissed my forehead, my nose, then ended
with my mouth. He leaned back and ran his
hands through my hair while he stared at me.

"You never cease to amaze me. I 'preciate the way you pay attention to me...and that female intuition shit ain't no joke cause you be on point most of the time. You worse than the FEDs girl!" We laughed out loud.

"Shut up boy! I just know you better than you obviously think I do. I know you ain't get that face card you got just by being the sweetheart you are to me. And You ain't make it this long in the game without a scratch for no reason either. I'ma a big girl Jabari I know this lifestyle is more than glitz and glam but I thank you and love you for not letting me see the other side." He grabbed both of my hands and kissed them, "Corinne I'm coming back to you baby....I promise." I knew this promise wasn't something he had control of but it made me feel better knowing he would try with everything in him. While we were talking Memphis and Monica pulled up beside us.

"Just enjoy yourself ok? Give me two hours at the most."

"Oh I'm definitely gone enjoy myself," I smiled, "You just be safe and come back to me."

He got out the car and opened my door. We all greeted each other in the parking lot then we kissed our guys bye and walked towards the spa. Before I went in I turned around and went to the driver side door of the car where Memphis was. Jabari had a confused look on his face. When Memphis rolled the window down I looked him in the eyes and said, "Bring my love back to me Memphis."

"10-4."He said saluting me then I turned and walked back to Monica who was waiting at the spa door. We both looked out the window and watched as they pulled off. Monica grabbed my hand and began mumbling something. I looked over at her and her eyes were closed. I realized she was praying. I hadn't talked to God since my mama died I didn't even think He knew who I was anymore. I had been so angry that he let her die that I just stopped talking to Him. I never stopped believing though so I bowed my head with her and said a little prayer.

God it's me Corinne. If you still love me and listen to me please just protect them. Don't take somebody else from me please.

We both said amen and walked to the counter. I could tell Monica needed to relax just as much as I did so we both requested the deluxe packages. Once in the back we both undressed and got ready for our full body massages. I gave myself a pep talk.

He ok Corinne. He promised. Quit worrying and enjoy yaself.

The massage therapist came in and got straight to work. I let her touch take my body into a place of deep relaxation but my thoughts stayed on Jabari.

Chapter 10: Jabari

I made a promise to Corinne that I didn't plan
on breaking. I promised her I was coming back
to her and by any means necessary I was
coming back. The way she was connected to me
always surprised me. She could sense when
something was wrong whether I said something
to her about it or not. She paid attention to the
littlest things and that had me captivated from
the beginning.

"Aye bruh how we gone handle this?" Memphis
asked bringing me back to the situation at
hand.

"Shit we finna let these niggas have it. I gave
'em fare warning." I said with a straight face.
Memphis cracked a sly smile; he was always
down for some pistol action.

HEART OF THE STREETS

Back around New Year's I got word from one of
the females in the apartments that some
Miami niggas had moved in the back and
was tryna set up shop. That was my hood and
me and my niggas was the only ones gone make
money over there. I caught the niggas outside
and told them *myself* the only way they could
make money over there was if they paid up first
and then when it was time to re-up they got
they product from me. Of course they was
happy to oblige that day, my pistol game was
triple theirs but I knew it wasn't gone be that
easy. These niggas was tryna make a name for
themselves. Fucking with me though wasn't
gone get them nothing but they name on a slab
somewhere. I kept a close watch on their
movements for the next couple of weeks and
stuff seemed like it had quieted down. Then last
night I got a call while I was setting up at the
studio, from one of my lil niggas in the
neighborhood, that one of my jays was helping
the niggas short stop. He was bringing them
jays to catch at the store in front of the
apartments. In the streets short stopping was a
definite sign of disrespect and I definitely felt
disrespected. One of the lil homies that worked
under Fatboy, named Carlos said something to
one of the Miami niggas that was outside about
it and a shoot out broke out. Nobody got hit but
it was the principle. These niggas was taking
money out our pockets and tryna cause harm
to niggas in my neighborhood. I let it slide by
letting them stay in the apartments period but
it wasn't sliding no more.

I grabbed my phone and sent a text to my boys:

Bubbas. 10 minutes.

Fatboy, and Bubba responded within five minutes but I was still waiting on Slim. He had been acting strange since New Year's with all that not answering the phone shit. I made a mental note and added it to the list. I was gone address that today too.

"You talked to Slim?" I asked Memphis.

"Naw I ain't heard from him since yesterday afternoon. He probably caked up though." Memphis said turning into the apartments.

"Shit it's Valentine's Day for all us too but business is business and this shit come first." My phone rung, "Call that nigga and see where he at," I said before answering, "What up?"

"What up bruh what's the move?" Yoshi said from the other end.

"Shit this party ours, I need to celebrate with bruh myself but I need ya'll to come help celebrate too." I said referring to the Miami niggas.

"Oh aight we in route to the party and we got all the big party favors with us." Yoshi said referring to the choppas.

"Yea cause this gone be a *big* party. Pull up on us at Bubba house in the apartments." I said

"Bet."

Click.

Yoshi and Dough was my niggas. They had been riding with me since a year after I moved up here to Atlanta. When I needed something handled on the North Side they came up and handled it and when they needed something handled on the Southside I made sure it was done. When I started moving weight I put a bird in they hands and they flipped it in 36 hours.

They was moving my weight like something off
of Blow. I set them up a trap house on the
Southside and they had been booming ever
since. I made sure they ate and they made sure
the bricks was flipped.

We pulled up to Bubba building and parked in
the back. When I came around the building I
surveyed the neighborhood. Nikki's kids were
outside like always but it really wasn't no
movement going on. The skies was clear and
everything was still like the world knew what
was about to occur. I picked up my phone and
called Sam the jay.
"Hello?"
"Aye Sam meet me at Bubba's."
"Aight Gunna....we...we...we straight?" He
asked nervously. Gunna was what my old jays
and the folks from the neighborhood called me.
"Yea nigga we good." I said reassuring him.
"Aight I'm on the way." He sounded relieved.
I was gone use Sam to draw some of
the niggas from the house to the store so I could
catch the other niggas in there off guard. He
was worried because he didn't know for sure if I
had figured out that he had been helping
the niggas short stop.
I got off the phone and called Nikki's oldest son
Corey over to me.
"What up Gunna? You heard bout the shootout
with them niggas and Carlos?" He said dapping
me up. He wasn't nothing but 12 and he was
already a product of his environment.
"Yeah I heard about it. Everything will be back
to normal soon youngin'. Aye do me a favor and
take ya lil brother and sisters in the house.
Make a round around the apartments and tell

all the kids to go in the house if they outside. Tell em I'ma buy them all ice cream Monday after school. Matter fact you went to school every day last week?"

"Yea I went but them white folks don't be talkin bout nothin'. They already got it in they minds that we ain't gone be shit so they don't teach us shit. So I be in the halls juggin' off these lil mix cd's I made and this candy." He said staring off into space.

"I hear ya lil nigga but make sure you go to class man. Soak up everything you can from them folks cause this street shit don't last forever. Beat them white folks at they own game with they own game. Graduate and be something then you can really shit on them folks." I was staring at him. I didn't have kids of my own but I took Corey under my wings.

"I feel ya Gunna but it's hard. I feel like all them teachers against me. They ain't tryna help me succeed." He said looking me square in the eyes. The way he said it, like he ain't have no hope for a future did something to me. I couldn't have these lil niggas running the streets like I did. The way the streets was these days these lil niggas was gone have a harder time surviving out here than I did. Soon as I got back to Corinne we was gone have to come up with something to help the kids in the neighborhood. I had to help them have some kind of future.

"I tell you what. You go to school every day and I'll set you straight at the end of the week. Bring me B's or better and I'll double it. Graduate and I'll give you 10,000. Graduate from college and I'll give you ten more," His eyes got big, "You down?"

"Hell yea nigga!" He said sealing our deal with a handshake. He was smiling from ear to ear. I reached in my pocket and peeled off a fifty dollar bill for him.

"Here, this for you going last week. But bring me something from the attendance office every week and ya report card every time it come out," I laughed as his smile faded slightly,

"You ain't think I was no sucka did you?" I was still laughing.

"Naw I know you ain't no sucka. I'ma do it though that check sound good." He said grabbing the money.

"Aight go head and do that. Make sure you go around the whole neighborhood." I knew once he told the kids the word would spread to their parents. I had more respect than fear in the neighborhood. It wasn't all fear like in most movies or stories of neighborhood drug dealers. I gave back to the neighborhood paying rents and bills for the single mothers that needed it, school clothes for the kids, putting food in the houses and so on. That's how I got them to stay loyal. If Cobb made rounds through the neighborhood or came to investigate, nobody knew anything. I hid my guns in different houses and cooked my dope in others. It worked for my operation and kept me under the radar.

"Aight," he said dapping me up. Before he got down the streets he turned around and yelled back, "Tell Corinne I said what up!"

"Aight." I said back. The kids in the neighborhood loved Corinne. She didn't come often but when we had block parties she came and would participate in the different activities with them. I loved to see her interact with the neighborhood kids. She didn't think she was too good to get out there and play kickball or jump rope whatever they were doing at the moment. I couldn't wait to make her a mother. I shook the thoughts from my head. I had to stay focused because it was time for business.

I walked in Bubba house and everybody was in the living room loading the clips and duct taping their shoes. Slim was sitting on the couch too.

"What been up wit ya phone bruh?" I said looking him in the face

He looked at his phone. "Nothing. What you talking bout?"

Everybody in the room kept doing what they were doing. They knew it was coming.

"You ain't been answering lately or you call back hours later. What's going on?"

"Shit ain't nothing going on. I be chillin' wit shawty or juggin"

"That ain't never stopped you from answering the phone before. Everybody jugg and everybody got a shawty but when it come to business all that shit backseat bruh."

"I feel ya.... I'm just tryna run it up like you." The way he said it made the hairs on the back of my neck stand up. There was a brief look in his eyes that I seen before when I was on the block with my pops.

"Nigga what that mean?" I said feeling tried. The room was dead silent. Money had never been mentioned like that in between us. Everybody knew a line had been crossed.

"Shit I'm tryna run it up like you." He said standing up.

I know this nigga ain't tryin me. Shit he can get his issue today too.

There had never been an issue between any of us but I ain't put nothing past no nigga. I turned and faced him head on.

"What bruh?!? What you wanna do?" I said on go putting my hand on the .45 on my side.

"Shit what up bruh?" he said defensively.

Bubba and Memphis got up and walked between us.

"Man ya'll niggas trippin!" Fatboy said from his seat.

"Ya'll boys man. Let that shit go and give it to these niggas in the back." Bubba said to both of us.

I kept my eyes on Slim the whole time I was waiting for him to make a false move. I loved my patna but it was a patna that got my pops killed.

Bubba pushed me towards the kitchen.

"C'mon bruh that's ya nigga. Ya'll cool off and talk about that shit later. Let's go burn these niggas so you can get back to my lil cuz." *Corinne. Damn I wanna feel her.*

The thought of Corinne calmed me down enough to let it go until after we handled them Miami niggas. I walked back into the living room to lay out the plans and Slim walked up to me with his hand stretched out.

"My bad nigga. You right I been slippin. My bad bruh." He said apologizing.

I stared him in the eye as I shook his hand letting him know we was good but I wasn't gone forget.

"We good bruh... just stay focused."

I turned to address the room.

"Aight ya'll. These niggas gotta go. I gave 'em fare warning but they wanna buck so we finna give em the business. Sam finna come

through here. I'ma have him call to get a rock
and when they go to the store to catch
him Yoshi and Dough gone be there waitin and
wet up whoever pull up to catch him. They
faces ain't known out here so they'll handle the
store. At the same time we gone hit the house.
Two goin in the back and two goin in the front.
Everything moving going to sleep. Who turn is it
to drive?" Slim through his hand in the air,
"Aight you gone have ya jay car waiting in the
back that's how we coming out. Then you'll
drop us off to our cars." They all nodded in
agreement.
My phone went off letting me know I had a text:
Back Door.

"Yoshi and Dough at the back door bruh." I said
to Bubba as I walked to the door and opened it.
They walked in carrying a duffle bag a piece.
Everybody dapped up and I explained the move
to them.
While everybody finished loading their clips and
putting on their gloves I walked over and looked
out the window. There was no one in sight. The
neighborhood was quiet which meant word had
spread. We were hitting these niggas in broad
daylight cause they wouldn't be expecting it. I
wasn't worried about the folks telling in the
neighborhood because we had been down this
road before.
I turned to Yoshi and Dough.
"Aye bruh...ya'll boys handle business and get
the hell on. Just hit me and let me know when
ya'll touch back down on the South Side." They
agreed, we dapped up then they left and headed
to the store.

In these streets you never knew when your next move was your last so we treated every move like it was; it's the life we lived.

It had been almost 45 minutes since I dropped Corinne off. I asked her to give me two hours and I didn't plan on having her wait. It was her Valentine's Day weekend and I was gone make sure she enjoyed it.

I looked at my phone checking the time. 1:32. I called Sam.

"Where you at nigga?"

"I'm pullin up now."

"Pull around to the back." I said hanging up the phone.

"Aight ya'll let's get this shit over wit. Ears and eyes open." Everybody got up and dapped up. I reached in one of the duffle bags and grabbed a pump just as Sam was knocking on the door. Bubba let him in.

"What up ya'll?" Sam said looking around the room. His eyes bounced from gun to gun.

"What's good?" I answered solely, "Look call them niggas and tell 'em you want something. Don't play me either nigga get whatever you been getting from them." I said with a straight face.

"Naw...naw bruh I aint gone play you. You my nigga." He said walking up to me with his arm outstretched.

My nigga. Hmph. This nigga'll set me up too for the right amount of dope.

So I wouldn't alarm him I gave him a closed fist dap, "I feel ya bruh. Look go'on head and make that call." I pointed at his phone.

He picked it up and dialed their number.

"Aye Marco this Sam. Sam. Yea. I need a gram."

GLAZE

These niggas slippin anyway making plays over the phone.
"How long cause I'm headed up there
now. Aight bet." He hung up the phone and
filled us in on the conversation.
"Marco said aight and that somebody gone be
up there in 10 minutes."
"Aight preciate ya." I reached in my pocket and
threw him a couple of grams that Fatboy had
sacked up for me. Sam's eyes lit up as he
turned and walked towards the back door.
Before he walked out he hesitated and turned
back to me.
"Aye Gunna we good right?" I could sense the
fear pouring from his pores. He knew I knew
something but he didn't know what. Far as I
was concerned if he was working with them it
wouldn't be long before he was willing to set me
up. I couldn't risk it.
"You my nigga right?" he nodded, "Well
you aint got nothing to worry 'bout. Go'on head
and head up there for them niggas leave out."
He turned and walked out the door smiling as
he looked at the dope in his hands. Sam had
always been a faithful jugg to my operation but
on that dope he didn't have a sense of loyalty. I
hated to see him go but jays came a dime a
dozen so I wouldn't miss him. I walked to the
window and waited for Sam to pull off. When
his car was out of sight I headed out the door
with my team right behind me. Business was
business and today we were handling ours.

Chapter 11: Jabari

I crept up along the side of the building and looked around; there was no one in sight. I cocked the pump I was holding and walked into the breezeway with Bubba right behind me. Memphis and Fatboy were at the backdoor waiting for us to make a move.

I pictured Corinne's face then my grandmama's. *I'm coming back to ya'll.*

I gave Bubba a look to make sure he was ready. He nodded. I aimed the pump at the lock and fired. The pump left a cantaloupe size hole in the door and we were in before they had a chance to react. Five seconds later Memphis and Fatboy were in the backdoor. Memphis immediately had to let a round off to hit the two niggas at the dining room table. I gave them a quick nod to let them know I was headed upstairs. I climbed the stairs and left a hole in

the nigga coming down blowing him backwards
into the wall. When we reached the top of the
steps I saw the right bedroom door close out of
the corner of my eye. Bubba had caught it
before me and was already headed there. I
watched his back and kept my eyes on the
bedroom to the left. He kicked the door open
and let off the M-16; I was right behind him
busting the pump careful to aim away from
him. Marco, the ring leader, fell slumped over
by the closet door gasping for air. He had his
.40 in his hand but didn't have a chance to get
a round off. I walked over to him while Bubba
checked the closets and the other room. Marco
looked up at me with knowing eyes. He knew it
was the end of the line. He tried to muster up
the strength to lift his pistol but I laughed and
kicked it away. I pointed the pump at him lifting
his chin with it.
"I warned you bruh." I said to him with no
remorse. I couldn't show emotion when it came
to these streets. He wouldn't have hesitated to
kill me if the shoe was on the other foot.
"F-Fuck you." He managed to get out.
I smirked and took his face off watching his
lifeless body fall to the floor.
Welp closed casket for you.
I turned around to find Bubba, Memphis
and Fatboy standing in the door way.
"Aye bruh we found them niggas stash.....it's
about 80 grand and a brick and a half." Bubba
said patting a book bag he was toting.
"Aight let's go."
We made it out the house managing to stay out
of sight as we got in the car. I knew it would be
a minute before them folks got called to the

apartments but I figured they was already swarming the store.

"Go the back way outta the apartments." I said looking out the back window. We could hear the sirens but didn't see any cops. I turned around and looked in everybody face making sure they all was straight. Knocking somebody off got easier to do the more you did it but it left a lasting impression on your memory. If you looked them in the face you never forgot their last expression. If they begged for their life you never forgot their last plea. I knew none of my niggas was scary and would let one off at the drop of a dime but even the toughest couldn't escape the mental torment murder could bring.

Ya'll boys good?" I asked looking out the windshield. They all answered with yea's and Bubba threw in a "You straight?"

"Yea I'm good. How ya'll left the downstairs?"

"I left the lil dope they was sacking up on the table and flipped the cushions on the couches so it'd look like a drug deal that went bad." Memphis replied.

"Aight. Well ya'll boys stay out the apartments for a couple of days till it die down cause ya'll know them folks gone be looking for any lil thing to bring somebody in on." Everybody agreed.

"Where the phones at?" I said looking at Slim. We never took our phones with us on moves so we didn't have to worry about nobody dropping theirs.

"They in the dash." He said passing the blunt he had waiting on everybody when they got in the car. I reached in the dash grabbed my phone and passed the others back. I sat back and listened to Jeezy's Trap or Die mixtape flood the speakers as I waited for my phone to turn back on. When it was finally loaded I had 15 text messages and 20 voicemails. I went straight to the messages from Corinne:

`I prayed for the first time today in 2 yrs. U were my first prayer. I love u Jabari. And by any means necessary u come back to me.`

I opened the next one:

`Are u ok baby????? I know u said 2 hrs but just let me know u ok....`

I dialed her number. I needed to hear her voice just as much as she needed to hear mine.
"Hello? Hello?" I could hear the uneasiness in her voice.
"Miss Lady I'm good." There was a silence but I could hear her breathing so I knew she was there, "You good?"
"I was just worried that's all," her voice was trembling, "Bubba with you?"
"Yea he right here."
"Can I talk to him?"
"Yea hold on." I passed Bubba the phone.
"What up Cee? Yea I'm good. You good? Why you sound like that? You ain't getting soft on me are you? Oh aight. We good and you know we got bruh. Love you too big head ass girl." I knew he was tryna change her mood and I appreciated him for that. He handed me back the phone.
"Yea. Where you at?"
"We came to Lenox." She answered.

"Damn my bad I ain't leave you no money."

"You good baby I got the money I made on the pole last night." She said laughing. It felt good to hear her laugh because it bothered me to the core to see her upset.

"Plus I got the money you give me every week. So I'm good I just couldn't function till I heard from you but now I can shop a lil bit." She said, I could tell she was smiling.

"Naw that's your personal money and this is your weekend so you aint spending nothing of yours. I'ma put whatever you spend back in ya pockets when I get to you. Matter fact grab you something to wear to dinner and go back to the room and get dressed. I'll be there soon.

"Ok baby. I love you."

"I love you too Miss Lady." I said ending the call. *Damn I love shawty with everything in me.*

We pulled into Slim's driveway and then around to the back of the house. He had a shed in the back where we put the guns until we could sell them back to the streets. We constantly bought guns so after a move we sold what was used to get them off our hands.

As we headed in the house Bubba pulled me to the side, "Aye bruh let me holla at you for a second."

I stepped to the side, "What up?"

"Corinne knew about that move?" he asked

"I don't hide nothing from her but I aint tell her about this one yet. Ya cousin got a way of just knowing thangs. She can read me like a book. Why you ask though?"

"Cause I know how you is bout trusting females. You really love my cuz I can see it on ya and when I talked to her in the car, the way she was worried....it just made me realize

ya'll genuinely love each other man. I appreciate
that bruh she needed you."
"Believe it or not Bubba I need
her. Shawty keep me focused. I'on even think
about these streets when I'm wit her. I can't
explain it bruh but Corinne got me captivated.
I ain't never had a female that put me before
herself.....she do it in every way. She make
me wanna be faithful....I ain't stuntin' none of
these hoes out here. They don't compare."
Explaining how I felt about Corinne to Bubba
gave me the affirmation I needed to make the
next move.
"Matter fact, look at this." I reached in my
pocket and pulled out a Tiffany & Co. box.
Bubba was smiling from ear to ear. The
expression he had on his face when he opened
the box let me know I chose the right ring.
"Damn nigga you did that! Cee gone love this
right here. How many carats this is?!?"
"3." I said proudly.
"I see you big dog. When you gone go 'head and
do it?"
"I'ma do it today at the Aquarium then take her
to the Sundial. I been walking round with it in
my pocket for about two weeks now
just tryna find the right moment. But I do want
ya'll boys there tonight if ya'll can."
"Well you know I'm there. I'ma bring one of my
lady friends...shit maybe two of 'em." He said
dapping me up.
"You hell." I said laughing.
As we were turning to walk in the house Slim,
Memphis and Fatboy were coming out. They
had already changed clothes and were ready to
burn the others.

"Ya'll niggas out here conversating and shit we ready to start this fire. I got a lil something, something waiting on me." Fatboy said when he got outside.

"Nigga it's conversing and shut up aint nothing waiting on you but a bottle of lotion and a flick." Bubba blurted out. We all burst out laughing.

"Nigga watch out!." Fatboy said laughing.

"Im'a go'on head and crank up this fire." Slim said still laughing at Fatboy. I still felt some type of way about the argument earlier but I decided to let it ride for the moment. He was my patna but that jealousy shit was deadly. I was gone sit back and watch his movements for a while.

Me and Bubba headed in the house to change clothes. We all kept extra outfits at Slim house for moments like this. I changed into a navy blue and white button down with the navy vest, and some khakis. I had on Polo from head to toe. I put on a brand new pair of Polo boots that I had bought a couple of months ago and never worn. As I was transferring stuff from my pockets I opened up the box and looked at Corinne's ring again.

She gone be my wife. My wife.

The thought alone made me smile. Just as I drifted off into thoughts of Corinne my phone interrupted.

"What up?" It was a girl named Keisha from the apartments.

"Hey Gunna them folks everywhere over here! They knockin door to door and everything. Ya'll boys stay outta here today." She blurted out

"Oh yeah? What they sayin?"

"They saying it look like a robbery/homicide. Just asking did we see or hear anything."

"Well shit 'preciate it shawty for keepin me posted. Keep your ear in them streets for me and let me know what's going on."

"Oh I got you. That's why I called to make sure ya'll boys was straight."

"Aight then shawty."

"Aight." We hung up the phone. I knew Keisha had a thang for me but she knew wasn't nothing going on.

I checked my messages. They were all from people in the neighborhood. Some were letting me know that they heard somebody shooting and the others were letting me know the police were in the apartments. The neighborhood was looking out for the most part.

I text Corinne letting her know I was on my way in 20 minutes then I headed out the door. When I got to the backyard everybody was just shootin' the breeze around the barrel Slim started the fire in. I walked over and tossed my clothes in.

"Aye bruh they say them folks in the apartments heavy." Memphis informed me as I walked up.

"Yea Keisha just called and let me know. She said they just asking if they heard or saw anything. Ya'll boys know how to play it...just stay clear til that shit die down. I ain't worried about it though...we been in this situation before." Everybody just sort of nodded and drifted into our own thoughts while the light from the fire danced across our faces. A thought of Corinne reminded me of what I was about to do.

"Well I'ma ask Corinne to marry me today." I said interrupting their thoughts.

"Oh shit! You was for real bruh." Fatboy said as a sort of question and announcement.

"Yea dead ass." I replied, "I'ma do it today at the Aquarium then take her to the Sundial...ya'll boys can come through if ya'll ain't got no other plans."

"I was tryna figure out what I was gone do about diner too...yea we in there." Memphis said referring to him and Monica.

"You already know I'm there." Bubba said with a smile.

Fatboy chimed in, "I'ma bring this new broad I met at 5 points. Shawty bussin' and her head game a fool. I guess I can feed shawty too cause it's a wrap after the holiday." We all laughed.

"What time we need to be there?" Slim asked. I looked at my phone. It was 3:04.

"I'm finna head back to the room and take her on one of them carriage rides to the Aquarium. I rented it out from 4 to 6. So ya'll probably need to be there round 5:30 'cause I'ma ask her at the end of the lil tour. They got it set up where the lights on the floor gone say will you marry me and they'll tell ya'll where to stand. Then we gone catch the carriage back to the room so we can change for dinner."

"Aight....my lil shawty wanna do a movie so we gone pull up before we head to the movies." Slim said.

"Damn congrats my nigga you finna be a married man....that shit aint for everybody! It definitely ain't for me." Fatboy said.

"That's cause don't nobody wanna marry yo ugly ass!" Bubba said laughing. We all joined him. Bubba and Fatboy stayed clownin each other.

We joked around for a few more minutes then finally headed to our destinations. I shot Corinne a text and let her know I was headed to her and for her to be ready.

We hit I-75 South riding to Goodie Mob's Cell Therapy. I couldn't wait to pull up on Corinne. I needed to forget about the streets for a little while and her presence was enough to do that. "Aye you nervous 'bout asking her?" Memphis asked turning down the music.
"I ain't nervous bout her being my wife but I aint gone lie....I'm nervous bout asking the question. But that's small thangs to a giant. I love shawty. I ain't never felt nothing like this before. Her loyalty the truth...shit everything bout her the truth. Real talk, she take me to another place....I'ont worry bout none of this shit when I'm wit her. She mine....I cain't even imagine another nigga putting his hands on her. She was made just for me."
"That's some real shit boy....and it's a good look. You ain't never been like this bout nobody. It surprised the hell outta me. Monica been rocking wit me for years but I ain't got the nerve up yet. I guess it's just that what if.....like this who I'ma be wit forever?....i'on know. But shit I'm wit ya. Corinne a good woman...you caught good when you got her."
"Preciate it." I said as we got off the Georgia tech exit passing the Varsity. We rode down Peachtree Street looking for the horse and carriage service. Because of the Valentine's holiday we found one within 5 minutes. I dapped Memphis up and reminded him what time to be there before I got out the car.

"If ya'll come through we gone be there at 4
and I'ma ask her round 5:45."
"You my nigga man; we gone be there."
"Aight. Later on."

Chapter 12: Jabari

As I took the carriage ride back to The W, I was consumed by thoughts of Corinne and marriage. I had a fear in the back of my mind but it wasn't a fear of marrying her at all, I was sure she was made for me, it was a fear of being able to protect her from the streets and the bullshit that came with the lifestyle. The streets was all I knew, the streets was me, but to protect her from it was to protect her from myself.

When I looked up we were in front of the hotel. I called Corinne.

"Hey Baby." She answered. All the memories of the day's events so far went out the window.

"What up Miss Lady."

"Where you at?"

"I'm down stairs...come out the front. You'll see me when you get down here."

"Okay here I come." I could hear her smiling through the phone.

When she walked out the doors a big smile spread across her face. The carriage driver and I were standing outside the carriage doors ready to escort her in. She walked up to me and stood on her tip toes to give me a kiss. That always turned me on; her small physique was so sexy to me. A couple that was standing off to the side of us waiting for their car to pull up, smiled our way. They both threw me a nod in unison letting me know I had made the right decision by picking her up in the horse and carriage. I grabbed her right hand and the driver grabbed her other hand and we helped her into the cab. I climbed in and we headed towards the Georgia Aquarium.

"I apologize for having you waiting." I said as we enjoyed our ride through the city.

"Like I said this morning baby you make every day feel like Valentine's Day so it's ok. I was just worried about you and I know you do ya thang everyday but it was something different about today. I could feel it deep down in my soul, you know what I mean?"

I nodded, "Yea I understand...we connected like that." I kissed her on the forehead and she snuggled closer to me as I put my arm around her.

"You love me Jabari?" Corinne asked looking up at me. She knew the answer but I didn't mind stroking her ego.

"You know I do more than I can ever explain or show." She smiled and looked up at the buildings. I admired her while she admired the Atlanta scenery. As I was watching her, her eyes got big and she was grinning from ear to ear. I turned to see what she was looking at and when I looked up we were pulling up to the Aquarium. "Baby!!!! The Aquarium! Thank you so much!" she screamed as she hugged my neck. She had been asking for months to go and she was happier than I expected. I loved having that effect on her. I got out and helped her out then turned to the driver.

"Aye man here you go," I said sliding him his fee, "if you wait on us I'll tip you a 100 per hour."

"You got it boss. I'll be right here." He pointed at the spot we were standing.

"Preciate it Dad." I dapped him up and walked to Corinne. I had never seen the man before but dad was a term we used on the older men around the hood so it fit. Corinne was smiling ear to ear with excitement as we headed towards the entrance and walked straight to the front doors.

"Dang I guess ain't nobody doing the Aquarium today....the lines empty." Corinne said not missing a beat. I just smiled and led her to the ticket booth.

"I'm here for the 4 o'clock slot." I said to the woman behind the booth window.

"Your name sir?"

"Jabari."

She looked at Corinne and smiled, "They're ready for you guys." She said still smiling at Corinne.

Corinne had a nervous smile on her face as we walked to the doors. There was a sign posted on the doors that read:

Private Party 4pm-6pm.
Will Resume Normal Business Hours
tomorrow.

"Jabari what's going on? She asked with a nervous laugh.

"I ain't want you to have to wait in no lines or have to worry about looking around people so I rented it for you." I informed her.

"The whole Aquarium Jabari!"

"Yea Miss Lady. It's yours till six because we got something else to do." I was feeling myself now. She hugged me tight, "You never cease to amaze me. I feel like a queen thank you so much!" She had tears in her eyes.

We walked in the building and were greeted by our tour guide.

"Hello Jabari and Corinne. Welcome to the Georgia Aquarium. My name is Ashanti and I'll be your tour guide for the day." She handed us maps of each exhibit and motioned for us to follow her.

"This way you guys." She led us to the center of the Aquarium where a bouquet of white roses was given to Corinne by another employee. Attached to it was a note that read: *These white roses symbolize how pure your love is. Thank you for showing me that real love does exist. - Jabari*

She turned to me and hugged me. The tears were falling down her face now.

"I love you so much baby and thank you for being the man to give me something to love." I wiped her tears away and kissed her. When I looked up Ashanti was smiling from ear to ear and I could see other employees looking from their posts with the same smile.

"Where would you like to begin the tour Corinne?" Ashanti asked.

She turned to me but I cut her off before she could get anything out, "It's all for you.....We can start where ever you want to."

She turned to her map and pointed to a section on it.

"Great that's our Tropical Diver Exhibit. Let us set the mood for you guys then we'll set out on our romantic adventure." We both looked at each other.

Ashanti gave a nod and the Aquarium lights dimmed. The room was lit up with pink and red projected images. The images were the words Happy Valentine's day 09', Jabari & Corinne, and images of hearts. Corinne's face was full of surprise and the tears were back. This was far better than what I had imagined.

"I love loving you Jabari." Is all she could get out. She fanned her face trying to fight off the tears. Instead of wiping them away for her this time I kissed them.

God I know I'm the least of your worries...hell you probably aint listenin to me now but I wanna thank you for sendin' me Corinne. I don't know why I deserve her but good lookin' my G.

We walked behind Ashanti admiring each habitat, laughing and talking to each other. Every now and then Ashanti would mouth me the time to make sure we were on schedule. Once we reached the underwater hallway Corinne was met by another employee with another gift. She opened the box from Tourneau and found the female version of the watch she bought me. The note attached read: *Thank you for being THE diamond in the rough. Our love is timeless. –Jabari*

Her eyes were big as I put the watch on her wrist.

"Oh my gosh Jabari it's beautiful! I ain't gone be able to stop crying!" she said in amazement. As I hugged her I saw a shark in the distance. He was gliding through the waters without a care in the world and with no fear, I felt like the shark. I was gliding through life just like him, with no worries and no fear. Just when I was about to turn my head a whale shark swam over the tiger shark I was watching and he was three times bigger.

Damn. No matter how invincible you feel something or somebody bigger always out there lurking.

We made our way over to the Beluga whales and to her third gift. She was handed a Michael Kors purse with a big red bow wrapped around it from another employee.

"Thank you baby," she said with all smiles, "It's so heavy!" She unzipped the purse to investigate and found 20 crisps bands and a note that read: *You're priceless but here's to the things that aren't. ¬Jabari*

The expression on her face let me know I had made her day and nothing stroked my ego more than to know I was the reason she was smiling. All of a sudden I wasn't stressing asking her the question; I was ready. I shot Ashanti a look that let her know it was time. As we headed out of the exhibit and back towards the front of the Aquarium, Ashanti asked us to wait conveniently by a railing overlooking the lobby. I turned Corinne to me placing her back against the railing. As I kissed her neck I saw my boys and their girls come in; Bubba was smiling like a kid in a candy store. The phrase: Will You

Marry Me? was projected on the floor in front of them big as day. I looked into Corinne's eyes and caressed her cheek.

Aight Pops I hope you watchin.

I grabbed her hands and opened up to her. "I love you so much Corinne; sometimes I wonder if I even deserve you. Nothing that goes on in them streets matters when I'm with you; you my breath of fresh air. I didn't think a love like this was possible but you show me every day that it is. You put me before yourself and you don't ask me for nothing. Because of that Corinne I want to give you the world and then some." She begin to shake as I grabbed her by the shoulders and turned her around. Her hands immediately went to her face as she gasped. I got on one knee behind her and took the ring out of my pocket. When she turned around she was crying with excitement. I hate to admit it but I had a little tear in my eyes too. "Corinne I wanna give you a piece of me that I've never given anybody...my heart. Will you marry me?"

Corinne got down on her knees with me shaking her head yes vigorously. I could hear my boys cheering in the background along with the Aquarium employees. Nothing in this world other than my grandmama mattered to me at the moment. The cars, the money, the street fame...nothing. Everybody came up to where we were and was clapping. I stood up and Corinne stood beside me as they all made rounds hugging and congratulating. When Bubba got to us he was the most excited.

"My nigga! Man I'm so happy for ya'll...I'm giving her to you bruh take care of my lil cuz." He said dapping me with a hug.

"You know I got her."

When he got to Corinne he picked her up and twirled her around. She was hugging his neck tight and crying.

"I told you Cee, Aunty was gone send you somebody to make sure you was straight at all times...I told you!"

"I'm so happy Bubba...I love him so much." I heard her say. She was staring at me while talking to him and I was lost in her gaze.

Pops.....she's beautiful man. She deserve the best and I'ma give it to her. I promise.

Today was the first time in a long time that I wished my pops was here with me. He had showed me the game but this was a total different ball park. I was so lost in my thoughts that I didn't see Bubba and Corinne finish their conversation or see her walk up.

"You good baby?" She asked putting her arms around my waist. I wrapped my arms around her and kissed her.

"As long as I got you I'm always gone be good Miss lady." We stood there hugging closely for a second with her head under my chin.

"Aye love birds it's time to turn up!" Bubba yelled

"Ayyyyeee!" Fatboy chimed in.

I looked at Corinne, she had so much love in her eyes, "You ready to eat?"

"Yes that's fine." She was all smiles.

"Aight let me talk to them real quick." She nodded in agreement. I stepped away and motioned for my boys to follow. As soon as I walked away Monica and the other girls rushed over to Corinne admiring her ring. All I could hear was ooh's and ahh's and see her beautiful smile.

"What up bruh?" Memphis said walking up.
"Ya'll boys still game for the Sundial?" I said as
me and Corinne was still eyeing each other.
They all gave a nod except Slim.
"Remember I told you shawty wanna go to the
movies." He said nodding his head at his date.
"Oh yea. Aight well preciate ya'll for coming
through."
"Already." Slim replied.
"Aye we can pop bottles in there? I aint got time
for them white folks to be acting crazy!" Bubba
had us all rolling with laughter.
"Boy you a fool!" I said laughing, "Yea nigga and
we taking the carriage ride back over there so I
guess yall can meet us. If ya'll get up there first
though somebody request a table for all us."
"We gotcha my nigga." Fatboy said smiling,
"You cain't even stop looking at shawty. I'm
happy for ya'll man ! I'm the best man though
right?"
"Nigga watch out! I done told you already that's
me!" Memphis jumped in.
"Aye both ya'll might as well quit while ya'll
ahead cause that's definitely me!" Bubba was in
the argument now. We were all laughing.
"Aye bruh just put me where you need me.
I aint finna argue with these fools!" Slim said.
I ain't know how I was gone choose a best man;
they was all my patnas.
"Aight let's head over there." I turned to Slim
and dapped him up, "Later on bruh...we gone
get up."
"Yea."
We walked back over to our ladies and then
headed out the Aquarium. When we reached the
spot where we were dropped off at, the carriage
was there waiting.

"Did ya'll enjoy yourselves?" The driver asked as we walked up.

"Did we?!!? Oh my gosh yes! I have the best fiancée in the world!" Corinne yelled out excitedly while she showed off her ring.

"Congrats young lady...I got something for you." He said walking to the cab of the carriage and grabbing something. Corinne and I looked at each other clueless to what he was about to do. When he walked back to the sidewalk we were standing on he had a sign in his hand that read:

Just Engaged!

with hearts around it. He showed it to us then proceeded to the back of the carriage to hang it up.

"Awww thank you so much sir!" she said squeezing my hand. He came back around the carriage and we helped her in then headed on our way. As we pulled off I felt my phone go off. I had a couple of text messages all from Yoshi. The first letting me know they made it back to the South Side, the second asking was we straight and the third saying turn on the news.

"Corinne....." I hesitated, "Im'a make this call real quick okay?"

"Okay." She said admiring her ring. She laid her ring hand on my knee; the gleam was blinding which made me smile at my taste in jewelry. The phone rang in my ear a couple of times before Yoshi answered.

"Bruh." He answered.

"What up boy? Ya'll boys straight?"

"Yea we good. You been watching the news?"

Naw I aint been round no TV today what's going on?" I asked.

"Shit they say somebody got to shooting at a store out there by ya'll. Left everybody but one stankin'. The passenger critical at Grady." He said informing me that they had knocked off everybody but the passenger.
Damn.
"Oh yea? When that happen?" I said for conversation sake. Never knew if the FEDs had a nigga phone tapped.
"Shit earlier today sometime..."
"Any innocent bystanders?"
"Naw them niggas just hit they target, but the news saying drug deal gone bad cause
the niggas drivin the car had a brick in the trunk and some choppas in the car."
The fact that drugs and guns were in the car was a plus for us. The victims weren't little innocent looking white kids on milk cartons. They were black and they were drug dealers. Them white folks aint care about us killing each other they felt like we were doing them a favor.
"Oh aight 'preciate you for letting me know bruh. What ya'll doin for it?"
"Shit I got a lil shawty I'm finna fall off in and Dough caked up now."
"Okay I see ya'll. Shit I just took that next step wit Corinne and asked her to marry me." I said putting my arm around her.
"For real nigga?!? He said surprised. "That's the move congrats my nigga! Aye Dough?!? Dough???" I could hear him yelling in the background to Doughboy,
"Aye nigga Jabari finna get married! He asked shawty today. Naw nigga dead ass." He came back to the phone, "Dough said congratulations nigga and he wanna be the best man."

I laughed, "These niggas up here talking 'bout that best man shit. Tell him preciate it."
Corinne squeezed my knee, "But
shit I'ma holla at ya'll boys later the misses' calls." I said mouthing okay to her.
"That's right take care of home my nigga. Later on."
"Later on." I said as I hung up.
My thoughts went straight to the surviving Miami nigga. He was either gone play police games or if he was really bout that life, want retaliation. Either way he had to be taken care of.
Corinne must've been reading me, "You good baby?" She was looking up at me.
"Yea I'm good Corinne." I said smiling trying to hide the fact that the streets had consumed my thoughts. She wasn't buying it by the look on her face but to my surprise she let it go. She just simply said, "I love you Jabari."
Don't let these streets ruin her day.
I grabbed her face and kissed her, "I love you too."
We enjoyed the rest of our ride admiring our city and waiving at the onlookers that honked at us in congratulations. When we pulled up to the Westin I called Bubba to see if they were already there. He let me know they were seated and waiting on us. I got out the carriage and made sure Corinne was in the lobby safely before returning to the driver.
"Preciate it Dad. Here you go and this for you." I said handing him his fee and an extra 200 dollars for waiting.
"Thank you Boss. Take care of that
pretty lil lady of yours and make sure she always feels appreciated more than just

birthdays and holidays. If she a good girl like she seem, she deserve it." He said in a knowing tone.

"She definitely a good girl and I'ma give her the world if she want it." I said looking at her through the lobby doors.

"I feel you...just don't forget to give each other the things that matter because when it's all said and done the material stuff gone pass away...but is the love gone stand?"

Dad was tryna spit some real knowledge to me and he had me thinking. If I lost it all today would Corinne's love be enough to sustain me? I turned and looked at her again and the smile she gave me made the world disappear; I had my answer.

"Her love is all I need." I said returning the smile. I dapped him up and walked in the lobby with Corinne. I thought making my first mil was the happiest moment in my life but at the moment I realized making Corinne my wife would be.

"Damn Miss Lady you got a nigga feelin on top of the world." I picked her up and spent her around, something I saw in the white folks movies. She stood on her tip toes when I put her down reaching for a kiss.

"The feeling is mutual baby. I'm one lucky girl." We kissed then made our way up to the Sundial to join everybody else. When we got to the table Bubba stood up and gave us a round of applause causing a chain reaction. He looked around and announced to the nearby tables that we were getting married. Before I knew it the whole little section we were sitting in was giving us a standing ovation. Corinne was smiling from ear to ear and as long as she was

happy I was happy. My team had bottles of
Moet waiting for us on the table so we all
grabbed one and popped the corks toasting to
our engagement. We enjoyed dinner and each
other's company continuously popping bottles
the rest of the night. By the time we headed
back to room we were feeling good and I was
ready to feel my future wife. We made our way
to the bedroom and through the maze of flowers
in the living room. We were so consumed in
passion that we didn't even make it to the bed. I
made love to her against the floor-to-ceiling
bedroom window overlooking the city. Every
orgasmic shake of her body sent me into a full
release and we went back and forth like that for
the next couple of hours. When all the passion
had drained out of our bodies we laid at the foot
of the bed holding each other. I ran my fingers
through her hair as the moonlight illuminated
her naked body. I kissed her then laid my head
on her chest as she ran her fingers over my
waves.

"Baby can I ask you something?" She asked as
she relaxed my body with her fingertips.

"Anything Corinne."

"When you asked me to marry you were you
prepared to marry me immediately or you want
a long engagement?"

I looked up at her and slid her body down so
that we were looking eye to eye. I traced her
eyebrow with my index finger moving one of her
loose curls out of her face.

"Why you ask me that?"

"Because I never believed in long
engagements....You know how people be
engaged for years? Well to me that's like a
layaway plan. Like they just asked the person to

marry them to keep them from going anywhere. I don't wanna be engaged for years or even months. I know you're my soul mate and you say I'm yours so why wait?"

Corinne's mama ain't raise no fool. I knew plenty of niggas that threw proposals around just to keep they broad campaigning with them. "I'm on your time Miss Lady. However long it's gone take you to plan out your wedding is how long we'll be engaged."

She took a deep breath, "I actually don't want a big wedding...maybe something little and intimate. When Mama was alive I did....but when she left that went out the window. I actually wouldn't mind just going to the court house and then since I don't have a budget, go somewhere exotic to celebrate. But I do know your grandmamma deserves to see a ceremony so what if we get married at the court house then have a ceremony later this summer or fall. We don't even have to tell anybody we already married."

I loved how she was thinking about my grandmama plus I was ready to call her my wife anyway so I agreed.

"That's fine with me Corinne I just want it to be a special for you."

"I know and I'm thankful for that. I'm looking forward to being your wife Jabari and the memories we create after." She said yawning. The day had been an eventful one I was dog tired and I knew she was too so I grabbed her hands pulling her up and towards the bathroom. We showered then I took the time to cater to Corinne's body; I dried her off and lotioned her from head to toe. This woman was my other half and soon she would be my greatest responsibility. I didn't want her to want for anything and I wanted to always be able to give her the desires of her heart. The thought of providing for Corinne took my thoughts to the streets. I was at the top of the dope game but the top was like standing on the tip of a double edge sword; it could all be over at any moment. The studio would be open soon but I had to invest in something else to keep the money flowing in. And besides the money I had to protect her from any physical danger too. I'd set the city on fire if anything ever happened to Corinne because of my role in these streets. The thought alone gave me goose bumps. I walked Corinne to the bed and pulled the covers back. She climbed in then I covered her up.

"You not coming to bed?" she asked sleepily.

"In a minute...you go'on head and get some rest." I leaned down and kissed her. As I got up to walk to the living room she grabbed my hand and said, "It's me and you Jabari til the world blow...I'm your backbone and best believe I'm watching your blind spot. You don't have to carry the weight of them streets by yourself...I'm here to share it with you. No pressure baby and no stress. I love you."

She was like the 8th wonder of the world to me at that moment. I leaned back over her as she lay on the pillow.

"I know you ridin wit me Miss Lady that's something I'll never question, but you leave the worrying bout them streets to me." I kissed the back of her neck, "and I love you more. Now Go on and get you some rest...I'ma lay down in a minute." She stretched out and smiled as she closed her eyes. I sat on the edge of the bed watching her sleep for a little while; she looked so peaceful.

I gotta keep her world perfect....this nigga gotta go.

I walked to living room and onto the balcony; looking out over the city. It was surprisingly warm for Atlanta weather in February and I had a perfect view of the stars with the clear skies. I never took the time to look at them but tonight they were extra bright and my thoughts began to wonder. All evening I had been trying to keep my mind off the surviving Miami nigga but nothing I did could shake the feeling I had. I knew this could go one of three ways: he could disappear on his own; I could go down the road, or it could end in bloodshed. I wished the nigga would just disappear on his own but my gut was telling me different. We got rid of this nigga whole team so he was gone definitely have vendettas against us. I had to either take care of him first or be prepared for whatever. With things going the way they were with me and Corinne I couldn't afford to wait for the war to come to me. I needed to meet with the team but I didn't want to take away from Corinne's weekend again so I decided on Monday for the meeting. I checked the time, 3:34 am, I knew my patnas were caked up or intoxicated so I sent out a mass message:

@ the studio Monday morning.

I never had to send out details when I sent a message with a location. They all knew it meant we were meeting about business.

Even though the hotel room door locked automatically I checked the door out of habit then headed back to the room. When I lifted up the cover to get in the bed I stopped and stared at Corinne's bare body for a second.

This mine to admire forever.

I got in and tucked her legs between mine as she snuggled under me. I whispered I love you and I'll see you in the morning in her ear before drifting into a dreamless sleep.

Chapter 13: Corinne

The Spring had treated us well; the studio was up and running and bringing in more money than we expected, the traps were boomin', we had purchased our first home on the South Side, and our love was growing unconditionally and uncontrollably stronger every day. His power is what drew me in, and my loyalty is what sealed the deal. We were built on a solid foundation and were now piecing together the walls of our future. I had finally given in and given up my job which of course made Jabari's day but I wasn't use to the empty hours so I started taking photography classes at Georgia State University. It was a hobby me and Mama shared before she died. When I wasn't in class I was making sure home was straight, the cooking and cleaning aspect, and keeping the books for the studio. And even though I had the

codes to the safes and access to whatever
money I needed Jabari still continued to give me
money of my own which i continued to put in
my savings account. It was our just in case
money. I never knew when the fairytale we were
living would be over and we needed to be able to
bounce back from whatever. By now the
account had an almost 7 figure balance
that Jabari never questioned or even asked
about. He knew I wasn't spending it because he
bought everything but I figured it was his way of
letting me keep a little of my own independence.
And even though he looked at it as mine I
looked at it as ours. I never understood how
women and men only thought of self when they
were in relationships. Jabari was my best
friend, business partner, lover, shoulder,
confidant...he was everything to me and vice
versa so there was no room for I in our team.
It was nearing the beginning of the Summer
and with two and a half months left before our
wedding Jabari and I were feeling on top of the
World. I had decided against the quick
courthouse ceremony and set a date for Aug 1,
2009, our anniversary. We were getting married
in Hawaii and would spend our honeymoon
there as well. Jabari's friends and Grandmama
were flying out for the occasion to represent his
side and Bubba, my aunt Renee and her other
kids to represent mine. Jabari was just as
excited as I was to have his closest loved ones
share in the moment with us. I was so glad to
see him smiling all the time again because it
was a sign that he was finally getting back to
his old self. He had been tense since Valentine's
Day keeping extra straps in the cars and at the
house, paying extra close attention to our

surroundings, buying me a new 9mm and taking me to the shooting range every week, and being strict on me being out alone. The thing I paid attention to the most though was the look of worry in his eyes that he tried to hide behind his sexy smile. I knew that something happened in the streets that day, I remembered seeing a news report about a quadruple homicide in the neighborhood he ran and another murder at the store down the street but I didn't question him about it. One thing I learned from watching Bubba was that no matter how much a street nigga trusted you, when it came to murder, details weren't discussed. And even though I would never pass judgment on him some things about his street life I didn't want to know.

On the beautiful Saturday morning of May 16th, Jabari finally let up enough for me to go out by myself. I wanted to go put fresh flowers on my Mama grave and head to my weekly hair appointment and I knew I had to catch him in the right mood.
"Baby I wanna go to Mama grave and then head to Alishia's to get my hair done." I said glancing over at him while he was sitting at the kitchen bar messing around with his phone. I was standing over the stove in a new pair of pink lace boy shorts buttering him up for the okay with a homemade breakfast: pancakes, cheese grits, bacon, link sausages, eggs and some fresh squeezed lemonade. When I didn't hear an answer I turned around to look at him but he was already standing behind me, boxers on the floor ready for his morning splash. I turned the stove off, relieved that I was finished cooking, as

he grabbed me by the waist and gently led me to the adjoining den where he laid my body on our white leather love seat and kissed me all over.

"Baby....." I moaned as he arrived at my womanhood, "Can I please....." but before I could get my question out I was sent into and world of orgasmic pleasure followed by passionate love making. When the love making was over Jabari laid next to me running his fingers through my hair. I loved when he did that it sent chills over my body.

"I love you Corinne and I know I been giving you the blues about going out alone...I just couldn't risk anything happening to you. That would kill me." he said with sincere eyes. "I know you have my best interest at heart baby so it aint no pressure." I said reassuring him that it was ok." But my next words sat on my tongue with hesitation, " Jabari you do know you can't stop fate though right?...I mean if something is going to happen it's going to happen no matter the amount of protection or guns." I watched him intently as he just stared off into space nodding his head in agreement. I knew he would always try to protect me no matter what but I also knew some things were inevitable. He sat there like he was debating with himself for a couple of minutes before turning to me.

"Watch your surroundings okay and keep your pistol where you can get to it easy in your purse. You got your license in ya wallet right?" He asked referring to my license to carry that arrived the month before.

"Yea I got it and I will. What you doin today?"

"I'ma head up here to the Barber shop then over
to the studio; Memphis and Fatboy layin down a
track today. Matter fact stop by there when you
get done so I can see yo' hair I like when shawty
do it."
"She do be having me on point don't she?" I said
while flipping my hair. I had been going to
Alishia's salon since Mama died; I couldn't find
the strength to go back to the one me and
mama went to together.
I heard Jabari's stomach growl reminding me of
the large breakfast I had cooked.
"I cooked all that food and we done let it get
cold!" I said getting up and rushing to the
kitchen to check the temperature of the
food, Jabari was right behind me.
"It's okay Miss lady," he said walking up behind
me kissing me on the back of the neck, "It's cold
for a good reason."
We both laughed and enjoyed breakfast together
then headed up to the shower. Once dressed,
I kissed Jabari bye and headed out the door.

We had acquired quite a few new cars over the
Spring and today I was in the 72' Nova that
Jabari bought for me. He knew how much I
loved Ol' Schools and surprised me out of the
blue one day with it. He had it restored with
black candied paint and Barbie Pink racing
stripes, black leather interior with my initials
to-be, C.W., engraved in the headrest and some
Rally's with pink brake shoes. The tag read:
The Mrs.
and it was by far my favorite of our cars.
It was a beautiful day outside and I was in the
mood to listen to some Oldies, so I let down the
windows and blasted KISS 104.1. I made my

way around Interstate 285 to the grave yard stopping by the local flower shop to grab Mama some fresh Lilies. They were her favorite flowers; when I was a little girl she always made sure the dining room table had a fresh bouquet every week. As I pulled into the cemetery and walked up to her grave I could feel her love all around me. I placed the flowers at the foot of her headstone and knocked away grass and debris that had found its way to her grave. "Mama I'm sorry I haven't been down here to bring you flowers," I said aloud as if she was standing beside me, "It's just been so much going on. The wedding is about two months away and I'm so nervous. Even though it feel like he already my husband that title means so much more....I just wish you were here to help me....I miss you so much." I whispered as the tears began to fall. "The only reason I'm even having a wedding is because his Grandma deserve to see him get married and I ain't wanna be selfish just cause you gone. But it is gone be small just his friends and his grandma and Bubba, Aunt Renee and the kids from my side. Since you left it just ain't that important to me....You remember that time we planned out my whole wedding? All the way down to who would sit where," I laughed to myself as I reminisced. "I know you would love him if you were here; he's so good to me Mama. I'm just worried about him in them streets...they gettin more ruthless by the day. I see why you always kept Bubba covered in prayer....." m y words died off as my thoughts went straight to where my relationship currently was with God. "Mama I know you disappointed in me as far as me and God go.....I stopped praying, I stopped reading, I stopped caring all together....I don't know if HE will even listen to me now," the tears came again this time in sobs, "I'm just so angry that he took you from me...He left me alone...You left me alone!" I screamed towards the sky not sure who I was talking to, Mama or God. Mama raised me to know and love God and to always keep him first but grief put me in a position of anger and resentment. I knew one day I had to get back to him I just hoped and prayed HE would receive me.

At that very moment the wind blew a newspaper AD around me a couple of time and then blew the paper against Mama's tombstone. What the paper said was enough to make me fall to my knees. The AD read:

Aren't you tired of running? Hurting? Feeling lonely or angry? God is waiting patiently on you. Choose him today while you still have the chance!

The ad went on to talk about some church in Marietta. I was stunned, it was as if Mama and God were speaking directly to me and my body was covered in goose bumps. This paper came from nowhere and out of all places landed on Mama's grave with the ad facing me, at the exact time I was questioning my relationship with God. I knew it was a sign that HE could still here me and more than that HE was still willing to listen. I sat in front of Mama's grave and wrapped my hands around my legs as I cried as if I had never cried before. It was as if I was releasing tears that I had been holding in

for the last two years. After the tears dried
up I began to pray.

*God thank you for letting me know you're
listening....I've been hurting so bad and I was
just so mad at you. Please forgive me for turning
away from you...I know it's going to take time
but I'm asking you to please ease the pain. Show
me where to begin with my life. Please just
watch over me.*

When I finished praying my hair was ruffled by
the wind reminding me of my hair appointment.
I looked at my watch, 12:15 pm; I had been at
the cemetery for over an hour. I got up blowing
a kiss towards Mama's tombstone and walked
back to the car feeling 10lbs lighter. When I got
to the car I took a look at my face and flinched
at my swollen eyes.

Damn. Where my sun glasses?

I reached in my purse moving the 9mm out of
the way as I grabbed a wipe to clean my face.
The touch of the cold steel instantly took my
thoughts to Jabari.

*And God I'm asking you to save Jabari .... Please
protect him out there. Bring him closer to you.*

Other than saying grace over our food, religion
was something we never discussed. I
knew Jabari believed in God, his grandmamma
made sure of it, but I didn't know if he was
saved or even wanted to be. We had never been
to church together and our house didn't even
have a Bible in it. At that moment I realized God
didn't exist in our relationship and I knew that
if we wanted to be blessed we had to invite him
in. I made a mental note to bring up God to
Jabari as soon as we got home that evening.
After being lost in my thoughts for a couple of
minutes, I crank up the car and pulled out of

the cemetery heading South of Atlanta towards Old National.

Once I reached the exit I grabbed a quick bite to eat then headed down the street to Love That Hair Salon and Beauty Bar; Alishia's establishment. I pulled in a front parking space so I could see the car from my chair and walked in.

"What up boo?" Alishia greeted me with a hug, her smile instantly lifted my spirits, "You good girl?" She asked referring to my tear swollen eyes.

"Yea I'm good just left the cemetery." I said with a you-know-how-that-go type of look, "Sorry I'm running late."

"Oh ok and no worries and no pressure boo. Let me get you back to wash so I can get you in this chair and relaxed." She turned to her sister Kylie, her shampoo tech, and motioned for her to shampoo and condition my hair. I loved me some Kylie, she was a ride or die type chick and was always down to buck under any circumstance.

"What up suh? Long time no see" She greeted waving her long pointed nails. I smiled and gave her a hug realizing how much I missed coming to the shop. I had become a loner after mama died and besides Monica, Memphis's girl, I didn't have any girl friends. Coming to the shop was like a hang with the girl type of thing for me and I enjoyed their conversation and company.

"We aint been seeing you..I know you ain't been playin' us for another salon" Kylie said as she began washing my hair.

"Naw girl, I just been wearing my hair natural." I said laughing.

"I was getting ready to say don't do us like that! How Jabari doing?"

"He good....just being Jabari." I could hardly concentrate on our conversation, Kylie was the best at washing hair and I was so relaxed.

"That's good I'm so happy for ya'll... you look so happy girl. When the wedding?"

"I am happy Kylie...he truly makes me happy and it's August 1. We gone get married in Hawaii." the thought of the Hawaiian sun on my skin made me smile.

"What?!? Ya'll better do that! Ya'll gone do something for the folks here that can't make it to Hawaii?"

"Yea we was just talking about that. We gone have something big when we get back to celebrate with everybody else."

"Okay just don't forget us...we gone turn up with y'all!" She said walking me to the dryer as she shook her hips with her hands in the air. We both laughed as other customers began agging her on with unison Aye's and Boaw's. Kylie was always somewhere dancing. I spent the next couple of hours playing catch up with Alishia and getting marriage advice. And even though she was a couple of months younger than me she was married with two beautiful children so I took her advice to heart.

"Make sure ya'll keep God first Corinne 'cause girl without God no matter how happy things seem the enemy got room to creep in. And remember Corinne, Jabari will be your husband not your boyfriend, you have to submit to that man....lift him up and be his backbone no matter what." I was soaking in everything she was telling me. I missed girl talk with Mama so much.

We chit chat for another hour or so, filling each other in on the ups and downs of our lives, before I was ready to leave the shop. I said my goodbyes and promised to come back in two weeks. As I left the shop I had an extra pep in my step, it was something about a new hairdo, a clean ride and the sun that had me smiling extra hard. I got in the car and immediately went to the mirror running my hands through my freshly blown out hair. It had grown so much over the last couple of months that the length surprised me. It was now down to just under my breast. I smiled knowing Jabari was gonna love my hair straightened and long especially since it was all mine.

Corinne...you beautiful girl.

As I went to pull out of the parking lot a small child ran out in front of the car causing me to slam on the brakes. A wild eyed woman ran after the child almost in tears and waving her hand apologetically. I was shaking as I opened the door to make sure the child was ok.

"Is he okay?!?" I shouted nervously.

"Oh my God! Oh my God! I'm so sorry! Thank you for stopping! Thank you for paying attention!" the young mother screamed as she ran over and gave me a hug. The young boy was oblivious to the fact that he almost got his block knocked off, he was smiling a gappy grin from ear to ear. I threw my hand to my chest with relief at his smile.

"Man I'm just glad he's okay!"

"You straight suh!?! Kylie yelled from the salon door ready to turn up. When I turned to answer

I saw that quite a few patrons had come outside to investigate what had happened.

"Yea I'm good." I threw her a face of relief and anger at the negligence of the young mother. "Man ya'll be careful out here. Watch them babies." I said with a concerned tone to the mother of the little boy. She just hugged the child and shook her head in agreement as her eyes filled with tears. I got in the car and had to sit still for a minute to gather my nerves. I couldn't even imagine how that mother was filling but on the other hand I couldn't imagine myself in that situation. I would always be on close guard of my children especially out in public around cars. The thoughts of the little boy triggered thoughts of my own future children. Jabari wanted nothing more than for me to spit out babies left and right but I wouldn't consider it before marriage. I didn't wait to get married to lose my virginity but I was waiting on marriage for children, Mama made me promise that when I first got my period.

As I pulled out onto Old National I called Jabari to fill him in on what had just happened.

"What up Miss Lady, you done?" he asked as soon as he answered.

"Yea I'm done you gone love my hair too." I said with a smile in my voice.

"Oh yea? Okay then. You on your way here?" he asked. Something in his voice was off.

"I was...why what's wrong?"

"I gotta run up to Cobb for a second and check something in the 'partments. You go'on head and head to the house and get dressed we going out to eat or something tonight...whatever you wanna do."

"Jabari what's wrong?" I asked ignoring what he was saying.

"Nothing, they say it's a car riding round the 'partments so I'ma go check it out then I'll be straight home." he said trying to reassure me everything was okay, but I knew better. If it was nothing he would have sent one of his send offs to check it out but he was going himself. Jabari didn't get his hands dirty unless he felt the person or situation was directly trying him, that's what his shooters were for. The pit of my stomach was in knots; something wasn't right. All of a sudden the day seemed gloomy but the same sun was still shining. A familiar feeling from Valentine's Day was creeping up but this time my gut was telling me it wouldn't end the same as the last time.

"Baby something don't feel right....something aint right Jabari." I said in a sort of hushed tone.

"Speak up Corinne," He said anxiously, "What you mean?"

"Can you just send one of your young niggas to check it out? Something about you going up there don't feel right. Please don't go." I warned. Jabari was quiet on the other end. "Aight go to the house Corinne, I'ma call you right back."

"I love you Jabari."

"I love you too Corinne." and we hung up the phone. I didn't know if he was going to take heed to my warning or go up there any way. I put my phone on my lap so I could answer as soon as he called and headed towards the house. About 10 minutes after we hung up Jabari called back informing me that him and his boys were headed to the house, I sighed in relief as we hung up a second time.

I turned the radio up to help calm my nerves and was so caught up in my thoughts that I didn't even notice the dark blue Impala following me.

Chapter 14: Jabari

Damn I love shawty to death. I thought to myself as I watched Corinne pull out the driveway. She was headed to the cemetery and I was headed to the barber shop. Her morning lovin' had me feelin' myself as I crank up the engine of my new 2010 Tahoe, I felt like sitting high today. I went on a car buying spree the month before just so I could switch up what I drove every day. I had to keep 'em guessing. I opened the compartment I had installed where the passenger airbag was suppose to be and placed my .45 in it. I had also tripled up on straps over the last four months since our run in with the Miami niggas. One of them had survived and instead of playing police games went back to Florida. When news spread of the murders word started traveling around the city about the head nigga, Marco, being the son of some Miami kingpin who was out for blood. My patnas with they ears to the streets brought the info to me and I was on go from that moment on since I didn't know where the heat would be coming from I wasn't sparin' no nigga. If you looked at me funny I was at your head, if you crept by slowly I was at your head. One thing I had learned over the years was that no matter how much love you showed the streets, the streets ain't show no love back, and I wasn't taking no chances. The thing that took a lot of pressure off me though was that Corinne was willing to roll with the punches. She ain't give me the blues about me puttin' the pressure on when or where she could go alone and it made it easier for me to move knowing she was straight. I took her to the shooting range every weekend for a month straight to get her shootin' game on point and to make sure she wasn't afraid of the kickback of any gun she might have to bust. To my surprise she was a natural born shooter; it ain't take her no time to learn. After I was comfortable in her shootin', I bought her a brand new 9mm for her to carry in her purse and made sure she stayed loaded. I never cared before how the streets affected those around me but now I cared how it affected Corinne. I didn't want her to be confined to a certain place and I ain't want her looking over her shoulders either. This was my lifestyle but I didn't want her to pay for it.

Once I got to the barbershop I just sat around shooting the breeze for a good minute after my cut. Niggas that knew me in the streets couldn't believe I was getting married and all the old heads was throwin' me advice. I let they advice go in one ear and out of the other though because wasn't none of them married. As I was about to leave I bumped into a girl named Carmen that I used to mess around with back in the day.

"Long time no see." She was tryna sound seductive, "How you been boo?" She asked reaching for a hug. I stepped out the way avoiding her grasp. Carmen was messy and she was some rip; I ain't want nothin' to do with that.

"Shit I'm good." I said as I kept walking to the truck.

"Oh you doin it like that Jabari?!? Fuck you nigga and that bitch you finna marry!" She was pissed.

"Shawty you wish you could be my bitch. Ain't you the neighborhood girl? Why you mad?" I laughed and got in the truck while she was attempting to curse me out with three of her kids standing beside her looking like what happened? I didn't have respect for women who ain't have respect for themselves. Carmen locked her kids outside just to sleep with niggas and had the nerve to try and turn up. I laughed again to myself and thought of Corinne. I realized how good of a woman I had. She was beautiful and loyal and I knew she was gone stand behind me no matter what. I couldn't wait to be her husband and definitely couldnt wait to make her the mother of my children. She had been fighting me about having kids from the time we got together and she wasn't budging. I understood though it was something she had promised her mama so however long I had to wait I would wait. Plus I enjoyed stroking her at all times of day and I knew that would change when the kids came along.

I pulled up to the studio 'round 1 o'clock to find Bubba outside on the phone arguing and Fatboy standing on the porch laughing at him. The driveway had a couple of cars in it so I knew somebody else was inside recording.

"Bitch i aint tryna here that shit! You knew what it was when you started fucking wit me!" Bubba yelled into the phone. He argued with one of his broads every other week.

"You good bruh?" I asked laughing.

"Shawty get off my phone," he said hanging up, "Yea I'm good that crazy ass bitch Kelsey talking bout she done fell in love and think I need to leave Tracy alone. What? Is she stupid?!? Tracy been riding with a nigga and she knew what time it was when she start letting a nigga hit."

We dapped each other up and headed inside.

"Aye who recording?" I asked Fatboy pointing to the cars in the driveway.

"Some niggas from the East Side and Dough done taxed them boys."

"Yea? Well shit if they went for it that's on them." I replied with a shrug.

The studio had two sound proof recording booths set up on opposite sides of the house so more than one group could record at a time. I went to the front desk and checked the cameras. The East side niggas was bout five niggas deep. "Ya'll watch them niggas."

"10-4" Yoshi replied already sitting in front of the cameras. Dough and Yoshi ran the security part of the studio for me on a daily and Corinne kept my books. The studio had the best equipment on that side of town so it brought a lot of traffic through the doors. It was pulling in more money than I thought it would and I was thinking about opening another location in Cobb. Corinne gave up her job for me and I was gone make sure her and my children didn't want for nothing.

Me, Fatboy and Bubba headed to the other side of the house to set up for their session while Yoshi and Dough held down the front desk and watched the cameras.
"Aye ya'll heard from Slim and Memphis?" I asked aloud. They both shook their heads no and Fatboy let me know Slim's phone had been going straight to voicemail since the night before.
Damn that ain't like bruh....he might not answer but his phone don't never go to voicemail for long periods of time. He stay with a charger.
I kept my thoughts to myself and called Memphis.
"Bruh?" he answered.
"Where you at boy?"
"Shit I was waiting on Slim that fool told me yesterday he was gone pick me up to come out there...that nigga ain't never showed. Monica finna drop me off though."
That aint like him either.
"Yea? You tried that nigga phone again?"
"Man I been blowin' that nigga up since this morning. Ion know what up wit that nigga."
"Aight well we all here...just waiting on you to pull up."
"Bet. I'll be there in bout 10 minutes."
We hung up the phone and I called Slim's phone.

"Your call has been forwarded to ...." I hung up and called right back. When I reached the voicemail again I left a message.

"Aye boy let us know something."

"That nigga still aint answerin?" Bubba asked going through his phone.

"Naw."

"I'm finna call the broad sister he fuck wit...you know I done hit her a couple of times." and he got up and walked out the room.

While Fatboy set up the session I couldn't help but wonder what was up with Slim. If he was locked up he woulda called one of and let us know. Something just wasn't sittin right with his phone going to voicemail. When Bubba came back in Memphis was right behind him.

"Aye the sister gave me his shawty number and she said he was with her til bout 3 this morning but that his phone been going to voicemail since he left her. She say she done called all the hospitals and jails and he ain't there." Bubba informed us. Everybody turned to me.

"She say she done called around so ain't nothing else to do but wait...bruh probably gone stroll in here in a minute with a million excuses" I said but no part of me believed my own words.

We had been recording for at least an hour when our phones started ringing back to back. I looked at mine; it was Keisha.

"What Up?"

"Aye boy it's a dark blue Impala and a black Taurus full of niggas riding around through the 'partments. I ain't never seen these niggas before and they asking for you." The words made my blood boil.

Them niggas gone try it?!?
"How many niggas in the cars?"
"The blue car full...like four or five niggas and the black car behind it ain't let down the windows so I don't know."
"Aight 'preciate ya for letting me know." I said getting ready to hang up the phone
"Aye Gunna?...."
"Yea?"
"The tags on them cars is Florida tags...you think them niggas up here bout them
Miami niggas that got killed?" She asked nosily.
"They still in the apartments?" I asked angrily.
You ridin round in my hood and bold enough to ask for me? They better be ready to get they issue.
"Ion know if they done left now but they was when I was outside. I came straight and called you."
"Aight preciate ya."
I hung up the phone and the look on Bubba face let me know he had gotten a similar call. Fatboy was in the booth and Memphis was on the phone in the hallway.
"Aye Jabari they say some niggas riding round the neighborhood on some fuck shit." Memphis said as he came back in.
"Yea we just got calls bout it....let's ride." I said walking past him and down the hall towards the attic. We kept a small arsenal at the studio and I was about to unload the artillery.
"Aye go shut that other session down. Tell 'em the studio closing." I said looking at Memphis, "Fatboy go grab Yoshi and Dough and fill them in." I said as me and Bubba made our way into the attic. I removed the tarp that covered the wooden crates that held the

weapons then took off the lids. The crates were full of choppas, pumps, bullet proof vests and bullets. I walked to the ledge and looked down to Fatboy who was standing at the bottom of the attic stairs.

"Them niggas still here?"

"Naw they pullin off now...they aint buck or nothin."

"It wouldn't have been a good day for em" I replied dryly. I was aggravated and on edge and ready for anything that came my way.

"Yoshi and Memphis pullin' the cars around." Fatboy informed.

I nodded in acknowledgment and walked back over to the crates. We handed eight guns down two by two and they were taken out to the trunks. As I made my way to the truck I could feel my phone ringing in my pocket. Corinne. I couldn't let her hear the anger in my voice or I knew she would worry. I leaned against the car and let the phone ring a couple of more seconds trying to calm down and then I answered. No matter how hard I tried to hide it she still was able to sense something was wrong in my voice. I didn't know how she did it but she did every time. Once I told her about the car riding around the neighborhood the next thing she said to me gave me chills.

"Can you just send one of your young niggas to check it out? Something about you going up there don't feel right....Please don't go." She was begging me not to make a move. The way she said it gave me an uneasy feeling. Corinne never begged me to do anything let along *not* do something. Even when her gut was telling her I was up to no good she would just always make me promise to come back to her. I was hesitant about answering her right away so I told her I'd call her back. When I hung up the phone I called a few people to see if the niggas was still riding around the apartments. The cars were nowhere to be found. I told a couple of my lil niggas to be on the lookout and let me know when they showed up again. I knew they couldn't be far and were probably waiting til nightfall to make another move. They were looking for me and I was gone make sure I answered them personally I didn't care who's son was who's and who had what status in the streets. Them niggas ran shit in Miami not up here and I was gone make sure they remembered that.

"They say they ain't riding through the apartments no more but we gone post up there tonight. I put lil Tony 'nem on watch till we pull up." I informed everybody.

"Yea we gone have to give it to them niggas this shit been going on too long." Memphis replied matter of factly.

"Aight Ya'll pull up at my house so we can get this shit together." I said as I crank up the truck, "And somebody try that nigga Slim again."

I called Corinne back and let her know we were headed to the house. I'd wait till we were face to face to let her know I was gone post up in the apartments tonight. I couldn't let another nigga handle this, they was looking for me.

Chapter 15: Jabari

When I pulled on our street for some reason I was on edge. I opened the secret compartment and grabbed my .45 putting one in the head and laying it on my lap. My gut told me to call Corinne even though I was a few feet from the driveway. Her phone rung and went to voicemail. I knew she was home I could see her car from the corner where I was parked. For some reason I wouldn't pull in the driveway and my mind couldn't grasp why she wasn't answering. She always answered even when she was in the shower. I called again.

"Hey Jabari baby." She finally answered but her voice was shaky.

"Why you ain't answer Corinne? What's wrong?" I said alert.

"Nothing baby I was taking a nap...guess I'm still a little sleepy. Where you at?"

"I'm on the way," I lied, something wasn't right. "Oh okay well hurry home so we can finish celebrating my birthday." She said trying to sound chipper. Somebody was in the house with her. We agreed that if she was ever in danger and couldn't talk to say it was her birthday.

"How many?" I said in a hushed tone in case they could hear me.

"Oooh yes! And I want eight new pairs of shoes too!" She said acting excited referring to the eight niggas that was in the house with her.

I know its them Miami niggas...but how? Our house is ducked off and only four other houses on our street. Nobody know where we live but my patnas.

"How they came in Corinne?" I asked careful to ask things I knew she could come up with an answer to.

"Baby and you left your stinky shoes in the foyer so I put them in the garage. Don't do that shit no more!" She forced a laugh.

They must've followed her in the garage.

Okay baby stay calm I'm comin...ain't nothing gone happen to you I promise! I love you! Do what they say...you remember where all the tools at right? Keep that in mind. I'm on the way baby I promise!" I had tears in my eyes. They had my heart in they hands and I knew they didn't care nothing about it but I had to keep her calm.

"Okay see you when you get here and hurry cause I can't wait to see you! I love you Jabari more than-." Click. Her phone hung up.

FFUUUUCCCKKKK!!!!! I screamed aloud as I punched the steering wheel. I couldn't think

and I couldn't focus. I had to get Corinne out of there alive even if I had to give up my life.
"They got my heart!" I yelled into Bubba phone as I reversed the truck up the street, "Where the fuck ya'll at?!? They got her!"
"What the fuck you talking about nigga?!? Who they got?" Bubba was just as hype as me.
"Corinne," I managed to get out.
Bubba's phone hung up.

I was standing in the middle of the street when Bubba's Camero came flying around the corner; he had to slam on his breaks to keep from hitting me
"Where my cousin at nigga?!? Bubba said jumping out the car before he even put it in park. Fatboy and Memphis got out behind him popping the trunk.
"They in the house with her. They think I'm on the way they don't know I'm here yet. Ain't no tellin what they doin to her I gotta get her and I gotta get her now!" I was losin it, "Bubba I gotta get her!" Just as I finished my sentence Yoshi and Dough pulled up.
"What up bruh?" Dough asked confused.
I ran past him to Bubba trunk and grabbed two AK-47's loading them with the 100 round drums laying to the left. I started towards the house not caring who was with me or who wasn't I had to get my heart out of there. When I got to the house it seemed extra dark even though it was a couple of hours left of daylight. Instead of walking down the drive way I went behind two of the neighbors houses and made it to our backyard unnoticed. I had to use the element of surprise it was the only thing I had on my side.

*God please don't take her from me! C'mon my G
don't do it to me!*
When I looked in the back door to the garage
there was the blue Impala and black Taurus.
*These fuck niggas parked in my garage! I'ma kill
every last one of 'em!*
I felt somebody behind me and turned to find
my whole team standing there.
"We gone get her back bruh or we gone die
trying." Fatboy said tapping the M-16 he had.
Everybody nodded in agreement except Bubba,
he didn't say a word.
"I'ma go in and go straight upstairs...ya'll hang
behind me that way if something shake ya'll can
have an advantage. Come out blastin'..... make
sure don't nothing leave breathin'..... watch
each other backs and stay alert." I took a
breath, "I love ya'll boys and if I don't come out
alive ya'll make sure she do. Take care of my
heart."
"We love ya too bruh and we all coming out
alive." Memphis replied.
I pushed the back door open. It was already half
way hanging where they had kicked the door in.
*They must've pulled in after they grabbed
her...she woulda heard the garage open.*
I made my way to the door that led to the inside
of the house. There was a stairway on the other
side that led to another door that led to the
main living room and foyer of the house. I
gripped the knob tight and slowly turned the
door knob so I wouldn't make noise entering the
house. When I was in I could hear their voices
coming from the living room upstairs. I crept up
the stairs with Bubba right behind me. When I
got to the door I took a second to listen. I heard
two voices talking amongst themselves; they

had to be standing somewhere by the front door most likely looking out for me. I couldn't hear anyone else which meant the others were in the living room to the left. All of a sudden I heard Corrine scream out in pain. The scream was so chilling it sent goose bumps up my spine. I burst in the door letting off a round into the unsuspecting niggas at the front door. The bullets tore their flesh apart dropping them where they stood. I slowly walked towards the living room glancing back to see Bubba standing at the door. When I reached the living room my knees got weak. Corinne was in the middle of the room leaned back in a chair. There was a cut above her eye and the blood was trickling down her face. Five niggas had their choppas pointed at me and an old head had a gold dessert eagle pointed at Corrine's temple. He had to be Marco's pops.

"Glad you finally decided to join the party." The old head said with a sly grin, "I see you done sent two of my lil goons on to meet their maker...I feel ya.... but now how bout you put them thangs down 'fore I blow ya bitch face into the front yard."

I clenched my teeth as I stared in Corinne's swollen eyes. She returned my gaze with a look of fear and helplessness. I laid the choppas down keeping my eyes on her as two of the niggas rushed over and grabbed them. One of the niggas knocked me to my knees with the butt of his pistol; I could feel the blood running down the side of my face. He put the barrel against the back of my head and dared me to move.

"I gotta give it to ya bitch though...she one tough cookie," The old head smirked, " I been beating her ass I know about a good thirty minutes, even let my son have his way with her....she still ain't tell me where the safes was." He said patting a dread head with a lazy eye on the back. At that moment I noticed Corinne's pants were pulled halfway down to the middle of her thighs. My eyes bucked and my nostrils flared with anger.

"You want me nigga! Let her go!" My words echoed through the vaulted ceilings.

"Tsk. Tsk. Tsk. You know how this goes nigga ... I don't just want you! I wanna watch you suffer first. What a better way to do that than to make her suffer? The thing you love the most?" He responded dryly. "You took my first born from me and today you gone pay for it.

I gotta give his mama some justice son, you know how *that* go." His sarcasm was making my blood boil. I heard the downstairs bathroom flush and watched a grin spread across the old head's face. Corinne was motioning for me to look with her eyes. When I turned to see who was walking up beside me my chest burned with hatred.

"Ahhh look who we have here...now ain't this interesting?"Marco's father continued on with the sarcasm. Slim went and stood next to the other Miami nigga in the living room. All of a sudden every word Corinne ever said about not trusting him came back to memory. I was usually on point about niggas. I could spot a snake from a mile away but I guess my own grass wasn't cut low enough....I didn't see this coming at all.

"Nigga you crossed me like this?!?" Like this? I put you on nigga! I fed you nigga! I put money in your pockets!"

"Nigga fuck you! You put money in my pockets why you the only one sitting on millions? Shit I got tired of being up under you!"

"Nigga I can't help how you flipped ya shit! And I been doing this shit what you thought you was just gone jump in and be on top?!? Naw fuck nigga you gotta put ya own work in!

"Aye both yall shut the fuck up....round here soundin like some hoes." The old head chimed in.

"Aye nigga I did my part...now pay up." Slim said to the old man. The old man just smirked and replied with a simple, "Right."

He kicked a black duffle bag from behind Corinne legs towards Slim. Slim leaned down and opened the bag pulling out a brick then cutting the plastic wrapping to verify that it wasn't a dummy brick. I could see the rest of the bag was lined with stacks of cash. Slim thumbed through a couple of the stacks and smiled a greedy smile to himself. Before he had a chance to get up the dread head beside him put the .45 he had in his right hand to Slim's head while keeping the choppa in his left pointed at me.

"What the fuck you doing nigga?" Slim yelled. The Old Head turned to Slim and said, "Let me give you a lil advice youngin: Never let greed cloud ya vision. You ain't really think I was gone let you live too? You went with this nigga to kill my son...plus you a snake. If you can't be loyal to the niggas that's been riding for you, you think I'm finna put some work in ya hands and trust you?" Then Old head nodded at the dread head.

Slim looked at me and all he could get out was, "Damn, my bad bruh," before the trigger was

pulled. Corinne screamed as Slim's lifeless body hit the ground with a hole the size of a lemon in his temple. The shot set off a chain reaction. Bubba and Memphis came from around the corner dropping the two niggas behind me before they even had a chance to react. Yoshi, Dough and Fatboy followed in behind them. Bullets were flying everywhere. I reached for one of the choppas on the ground and felt the sting of hot metal ripping threw my chest. The breath was knocked out of me as I was hit another time. I searched the room wildly for Corinne as I finally was able to grab a choppa and let off continuous rounds. When I saw Marco's pops body drop I stopped shooting and fell to my knees myself. It was getting harder to breath and my chest and legs were burning with pain. I looked for Corinne as I fell to the ground spotting her bloody body laying on the kitchen tile motionless. As I fought for air, flash backs of my life played like a movie. I thought of my Daddy and life before I knew about the drugs. *Damn I ain't think it was gone end like this. God if you can hear me don't take her life...She don't deserve this. Take mine and let her live.......*
I could feel my heart beatin' slower and slower and I was choking on blood just to breathe. I closed my eyes and lay ready to see what eternity had in store for me.

<u>Chapter 16: Corinne</u>

*I'm dying. God please! I'm dying. This can't be
how it ends. God, I haven't lived yet! I can't go
like this...Please God, Please!*
I played the events over and over in my head as
my bullet riddled body lay in a pool of blood and
shattered glass. Every warning Jabari had ever
given me about watching my surroundings and
checking if someone was following me was
ringing loudly in my ears.
If I had just paid attention!
I didn't know how long they had been following
me or where they had even followed me from
but by the time I noticed them I was on our
street and they were pulling in the driveway
behind me. I tried to stay in the car but the one
with the dreads bust my window and had
a choppa in my face before I could even reach
for my gun. He pulled me out of the car by my

hair and they forced me in the house. The older man let me know why they were there and what had happened to his son. I knew from that moment I was going to die today. I had already messed up by letting them follow me to the house so when they started asking where the safes were I wouldn't budge. They were going to kill me anyway I wasn't gone let them kill me and take the money. Even after the older man started beating me and the dread head raped me I still wouldn't tell them. I just imagined I was somewhere else to keep my mind off of what was happening to me. When Jabari showed up all I could do was watch and pray they didn't kill him in front of me because seeing them kill Slim was traumatizing enough. Choking on my own blood brought me out of my thoughts and back to the position I was in. I had to find Jabari and get help.

Get up Corinne. Get up. You have to get up. I told myself. The chill from the tiles on the floor began to make me shiver. My breathing became shallow.

Not like this Corinne! Get yourself together. Get Up! Get Up!

I gathered enough strength to turn on my side but what I saw caused more pain than the four bullets that had ripped my flesh apart. Less than four feet from me on the living room floor was his body. Bloody and still. All of a sudden the room became cold and hard.

"Baby! Baby! Jabari please open your eyes!" I tried to scream, "Open your eyes baby!" I pleaded tearfully.

God please don't do this. Please don't let him be dead. Please don't let me die. God please!

With the smell of gun powder burning my nose,
I began to make my way to Jabari's motionless
body, every movement causing more and more
affliction. I climbed through a massive sea of
hot shells and still bodies and after what
seemed like an eternity I was finally close
enough to lay my head on his blood spattered
chest.

"Jabari baby please just open your eyes!
Please," I begged.

The smell of burnt flesh clouded my nostrils,
overtaking the gun powder smell of the room. I
could feel Jabari's warm blood ooze from his
chest beneath my blood stain cheeks. I inched
closer to his face to see if I could see a sign of
life. There was nothing.

Please God let there be a heartbeat. God
answered immediately.

Boom Boom.....Boom Boom.... It was weak but
it was there. I closed my eyes in prayer.

God please!

There was a faint sound.

God please!

The sound became clearer.

"Corinne," he struggled to get out, "Corinne."

"I'm here baby! Please open your eyes. Just let
me see your eyes!"

Jabari's eyes began to flutter and slowly
opened. He mustered enough strength to look at
me for what felt like would be the last time.

"I'm...I'm sorry...I'm so sorry," Jabari said
through clenched teeth; His pain seemed
unbearable.

"Don't apologize baby, it's all my fault!...it's my
fault! Please just hold on. It's me and you till
the end right?" He shook his head yes, "Okay

then this ain't our end! Hold on Jabari please," I begged still choking on my own blood.

I laid my hands on his wounds and began to pray.

God please help us. I'm sorry God....we're sorry! Please don't let it end like this. If you spare us from this death God my life is yours! I promise God, I promise.

I felt movement. Jabari's hand had found mine like many times before and we held on to each other. However, something was very different about this time; we were literally holding on for dear life.

I knew I had to find a phone and call for help. I tried reaching in Jabari's pocket but his wasn't there. With each movement I struggled to breath but I pushed through the pain for me and Jabari's sake.

God please help me find a phone....please help me.

All of a sudden I could hear the muffled sounds of a phone ringing from one of the bodies lying in the hallway. The thought of getting the phone off of a dead body tried to send fear through my bones but my will to live overcame the feeling. I kissed Jabari's cheek and begged him to hold on, "I'm going to get us help baby...hold on for me." His breathing was getting fainter by the minute and the familiar agonizing pain of watching someone you loved die begin to slowly creep in.

I inched my way over the man's stiff body only to recognize a familiar tattoo on his arm. It was the cross Fatboy has gotten for his grandmother earlier that year. My eyes stung with tears over Fatboy's death, he and Jabari had been rockin' since Jabari moved to Atlanta, I knew he would miss him. I reached in his blood stain jeans and pulled his phone out dialing 911 with my trembling fingers.

"9-1-1. What's your emergency?"

"Please hurry there's been a shooting...I've been shot....he got shot....please hurry!" I blurted out at the sound of the young woman's voice.

"Ma'am I need you to calm down...where is the gunman?" She asked in a soothing voice.

"I don't know I think they're dead....please hurry!"

"I have the police on the way ma'am...where are you shot?"

I felt around for the holes, "I don't know I think in the leg and stomach....please just hurry!" I began to cry.

"You have to stay calm ma'am...how many others are shot?"

I lifted my head as high as I could and surveyed the entire scene for the first time. The sight of all the bodies was horrific but the thing that caused the most pain was laying eyes on Bubba. I cried out in grief.

"Bubba please come back! God please send him back!" The hole in the middle of his head let me know my prayers would go unanswered.

"They killed him! They killed my cousin! It's my fault....it's my fault!" I cried hysterically.

I was physically and emotionally dying and I no longer cared about the operator on the line or even had the energy to hold the phone. If it was God's will for me to live, they would come in time. If it wasn't His will, I prayed He took my soul. I dropped the phone and tried to inch my way back over to Jabari but all my strength was gone, I just laid there hoping and praying for the best.

After I had been in and out of consciousness for what seemed like a lifetime I saw the glow of flashlights shining all around me. Help had finally come but my heart was telling me they had come too late. As the paramedics began loading me on to the gurney and making their way around the room I heard one yell "I have a pulse!" then another one yelled "One over here too." The neck brace I was wearing wouldn't allow me to turn to see who they were talking about but I prayed with all my might one of them was Jabari.

Chapter 17: One Year Later

It had been exactly one year since that life changing day and I stopped by Mama and Bubba's graves to pay my respects. The year had been a rough one emotionally but I was at my strongest spiritually. I smirked at how God uses our worst and weakest moments to bring us to him. Like He's saying, "By any means necessary I'ma save you my child." I spent that year finding my way to him and learning how to keep him first. Before that fateful day, God didn't have a position in my life and I learned the hard way a life without God was simply a life with the enemy.

A couple of weeks after the shooting the FEDs conducted an investigation. They seized all of our possessions and assets but because there wasn't a paper trail they didn't have enough evidence for criminal charges so none were filed. The only account left untouched was my personal account which, thanks to Jabari's weekly blessings and my savings, had a little over a million dollars in it. So even though we took a loss, it wasn't a total loss.

I snapped out of my reminiscent thoughts and leaned down to placed a bouquet of flowers on each of their graves wishing badly they were still alive to smell them. I still felt a sense of guilt about Bubba's death, it was an issue I had to give to God daily, but I was getting through it. As I knelt at Bubba's headstone my vision became blurry from the tears that were fighting to be released, but before one could fall I felt a hand touch my back and turned around to find Jabari standing behind me. He had gotten out of the car and decided to join me in paying respects. He grabbed my hand and asked was I okay then turned and faced his patnas grave for the first time since his death. We both stood there in silence holding on to each other for support wishing we could rewind time. I removed my hand from his grasp and wrapped it around his waist as I watched him intently. That unforgettable day Jabari lost everybody in his crew but one, Memphis, and as grief tried to make him bitter I watched God make him stronger. There was a change in the man standing beside me. Not only had he given his life to God but now he had a new sense of how precious life was. He walked away from the streets with five bullet wounds and empty handed but he was able to keep his life and I thanked God for saving him physically and spiritually every day.

As his tears silently fell I rubbed his back and said a quick prayer.

God I'm asking you to give him the strength to push through his grief today and please restore his joy.

We stood out there for another 30 minutes or so before we started heading back to the car. As we walked, Jabari stepped behind me and wrapped his arms around my stomach. I was 6 months pregnant with our first child and he was more than excited.

"Corinne?"

"Yes Baby?"

"I love you and I'm glad you finally my wife."

I smiled and twirled my ring around my finger, "I am too and I'm glad that you're my husband."

After walking me to my side of the car, he took one last look at Bubba's grave then got in the car. After driving in silence for a couple of seconds, Jabari finally spoke up.

"I had to go through death to find life..... and no matter how much it hurts I'm thankful because now I can love you the way a man should and instead of giving my son the game I can give him God."

I grabbed his hand and smiled as I rubbed my belly with the other. I was amazed at what God was doing in our lives. He had stripped us of everything only to give us more than we really ever had. And no matter the pain that we had to go through to get to Him, the fact that He still loved us enough to give us another chance was satisfaction enough for us. We had God, We had each other, and in a few months we would have a son. I was overwhelmed with joy and as we drove into the sunset I looked at the sky and simply said, "God, you did that!"

HEART OF THE STREETS

GLAZE

ABOUT THE AUTHOR

Chenae Glaze is a talented author whose passion for reading led her to her passion for writing. She is a born again Christian who relies on her Faith in all situations. Chenae was born in Marietta, Ga. where she currently resides.

Made in the USA
Columbia, SC
10 May 2020